THWICK!
BANG
BANG
BOOM!

Hi, I'm JIMMY!

Like me, you probably noticed the world is run by adults.

But ask yourself: Who would do the best job

of making books that *kids* will love?

Yeah. **Kids!**

So that's how the idea of JIMMY books came to life.

We want every JIMMY book to be so good

that when you're finished, you'll say,

"PLEASE GIVE ME ANOTHER BOOK!"

Give this one a try and see if you agree.

(If not, you're probably an adult!)

JIMMY PATTERSON BOOKS FOR YOUNG READERS

JAMES PATTERSON PRESENTS

Sci-Fi Junior High by John Martin and Scott Seegert
Sci-Fi Junior High: Crash Landing by John Martin and Scott Seegert
How to Be a Supervillain by Michael Fry
How to Be a Supervillain: Born to Be Good by Michael Fry
The Unflushables by Ron Bates

THE MIDDLE SCHOOL SERIES BY JAMES PATTERSON

Middle School: The Worst Years of My Life
Middle School: Get Me Out of Here!
Middle School: Big Fat Liar
Middle School: How I Survived Bullies, Broccoli, and Snake Hill
Middle School: Ultimate Showdown
Middle School: Save Rafe!
Middle School: Just My Rotten Luck
Middle School: Dog's Best Friend
Middle School: Escape to Australia
Middle School: From Hero to Zero

THE I FUNNY SERIES BY JAMES PATTERSON

I Funny
I Even Funnier
I Totally Funniest
I Funny TV
I Funny: School of Laughs

THE TREASURE HUNTERS SERIES BY JAMES PATTERSON

Treasure Hunters
Treasure Hunters: Danger Down the Nile
Treasure Hunters: Secret of the Forbidden City
Treasure Hunters: Peril at the Top of the World
Treasure Hunters: Quest for the City of Gold

THE HOUSE OF ROBOTS SERIES BY JAMES PATTERSON

House of Robots
House of Robots: Robots Go Wild!
House of Robots: Robot Revolution

THE DANIEL X SERIES BY JAMES PATTERSON

The Dangerous Days of Daniel X
Daniel X: Watch the Skies
Daniel X: Demons and Druids
Daniel X: Game Over
Daniel X: Armageddon
Daniel X: Lights Out

OTHER ILLUSTRATED NOVELS AND STORIES

Laugh Out Loud
Pottymouth and Stoopid
Jacky Ha-Ha
Jacky Ha-Ha: My Life Is a Joke
Word of Mouse
Public School Superhero
Give Please a Chance
Give Thank You a Try
Big Words for Little Geniuses
The Candies Save Christmas

For exclusives, trailers, and other information, visit jamespatterson.com.

TREASURE HUNTERS

QUEST FOR THE CITY OF GOLD

BY JAMES PATTERSON

AND CHRIS GRABENSTEIN

ILLUSTRATED BY

JULIANA NEUFELD

JIMMY PATTERSON BOOKS

LITTLE, BROWN AND COMPANY

NEW YORK BOSTON LONDON

JIMMY Patterson Books / Little, Brown and Company
Hachette Book Group
1290 Avenue of the Americas, New York, NY 10104
jamespatterson.com

First Edition: January 2018

JIMMY Patterson Books is an imprint of Little, Brown and Company, a division of Hachette Book Group, Inc. The Little, Brown name and logo are trademarks of Hachette Book Group, Inc. The JIMMY Patterson Books® name and logo are trademarks of JBP Business, LLC.

Library of Congress Cataloging-in-Publication Data
Patterson, James, author. | Grabenstein, Chris, author. |
Neufeld, Juliana, illustrator.
Title: Quest for the city of gold / by James Patterson and Chris Grabenstein; illustrated by Juliana Neufeld.
Description: First edition. | New York ; Boston : Little, Brown and Company, 2017. | Series: Treasure hunters ; 5 | Summary: Twins Bick and Beck Kidd and their family of professional treasure hunters race against mercenaries, rival treasure hunters, and a lumber baron through the jungles and mountains of Peru in search of Paititi, the legendary lost Inca city of gold, in hope of conserving the archaeological treasure and preventing deforestation of the rain forest.
LCCN 2016052585 | ISBN 978-0-316-34955-0 (paper over board)
Adventure and adventurers—Fiction. | Buried treasure—Fiction. | Brothers and sisters—Fiction. | Twins—Fiction. | Family-owned business enterprises—Fiction. | Peru—Fiction.
LCC PZ7.P27653 Qu 2017 | DDC [Fic]—dc23

10 9 8 7 6 5 4 3 2 1

LSC-H

Printed in the United States of America

For Will Hunt, who found his own treasure: Reading

GREENLAND

MUSK-OXEN

NORTH AMERICA

THE UNITED STATES

ATLANTIC OCEAN

MEXICO

TIP: JAGUARS HATE SNAKES AS MUCH AS WE DO.

CENTRAL AMERICA

ARENAL VOLCANO

COSTA RICA

COCOS ISLAND

TIP: WATCH OUT FOR HAMMERHEAD SHARKS!

AMAZON

THE WORLD'S BIGGEST RAIN FOREST. VERY EASY TO GET LOST IN...

PERU

CUZCO

HOME TO SOME SERIOUSLY QUESTIONABLE FOODS. GRILLED GUINEA PIG, ANYONE?

SOUTH AMERICA

THE WORLD AC

ARCTIC OCEAN

RUSSIA

★ ST. PETERSBURG

WHERE BICK AND I *ALMOST* HAD TWIN TIRADE #609. MOM'S AND DAD'S GLARES WERE SCORCHING. YOWZA!

OPE

WHERE MOM FOUND THE *TUMI* KNIFE. CHE FORTUNA!

ASIA

CHINA

PANDAS SPEND 14 TO 16 HOURS A DAY EATING... JUST LIKE BICK.

PACIFIC OCEAN

RICA

INDONESIA DOESN'T KNOW HOW MANY ISLANDS IT CONTAINS. 17,508, 17,509, 17,510...

INDIAN OCEAN

GROUND NGOLIN

ZAMBIA

VICTORIA FALLS

ZIMBABWE

A QUOKKA!

AUSTRALIA

SOUTHERN OCEAN

TO THE KIDDS!

RCTICA

QUICK NOTE FROM BICK KIDD

Before we dive into our next adventure—and I mean literally dive, because it starts with Beck and me swimming for our lives—I just want to remind everybody that I, Bickford "Bick" Kidd, will be the one telling this tale.

My twin sister, Rebecca "Beck" Kidd, will be handling the drawings.

I'm the author, she's the illustrator.

I'm the narrator, she's the picture scribbler.

Fine. Beck says I'm also the stinky one and she's the one who doesn't smell like ancient cheese stuffed into gym socks.

Whatever.

It's time to jump into the story.

And the shark-infested waters.

Part I

Pirate Treasure

THE SHARKS MUST THINK WE'RE FISH!

PROBABLY BECAUSE THEY SMELLED YOUR FEET!

CHAPTER 1

Okay, to start, I have to admit that I'm seriously impressed by my twin sis Beck's ability to draw that picture, because at the time, we were maybe ten seconds away from being chomped on by a family of hammerhead sharks.

(Beck says she drew that illustration later on, from memory, not while we were in the water. I'm doing the same thing with the storytelling. It's hard to write or draw while you're swimming for your life. The ink gets all runny and splotchy.)

Where were we?

Oh, right. In the ocean. Off the coast of Costa Rica. Being chased by hammerhead sharks as we swam our way to Cocos Island, a Costa Rican national park also known as "the Island of Sharks."

(Yes, Beck, that *should* have been a hint as to what might be lurking beneath the waves.)

We furiously paddled our arms and kicked our legs and tried to outrun the swarm of hungry sea monsters. Good thing hammerheads have eyeballs where their ears should be. Maybe they couldn't see us—*swimming right in front of them.*

Why weren't we in a rowboat or a motorized raft?

Because Mom, Dad, and our big brother, Tommy, had taken all available landing craft when they decided to do a little treasure hunting on Cocos Island without me, Beck, or our big sister, Storm.

"You three need to stay with the ship," Dad

had said when they loaded up the boats. "There are secrets belowdecks in the Room you need to guard."

Yes, whenever Dad talks about the Room, it sounds like he's capitalizing it, because the Room is this super-secret high-security walk-in vault on our ship, the *Lost*. The Room is off-limits to all of us. It's where Mom and Dad keep their rare and valuable treasure-hunting maps locked up behind the Door. The Door gets the capital-letter treatment, too, because it's made out of three-inch-thick solid steel. It's so heavy I sometimes wonder how the *Lost* can stay afloat with that much deadweight in its hull.

I was pretty sure Beck and I had remembered to double-check the lock on the Door to the Room before we jumped into the Ocean. Pretty sure. We were kind of in a rush.

"How dare they go looking for the Treasure of Lima without us!" Beck had said as we prepared to dive in.

"Yeah," I'd said. "How dare they!"

Yes, we sometimes think and say exactly the same stuff. It's a twin thing.

So we jumped overboard and started swimming. Don't forget, we Kidd kids have lived on the ocean most of our lives. We're excellent swimmers and scuba divers. Except Storm. She doesn't do water sports. Maybe because she has a photographic memory, which means that she never forgets that the ocean is full of scary creatures like, oh, hammerhead sharks!

But Beck and I were determined to join Mom, Dad, and Tommy on the island. Hey, we Kidd kids did pretty well treasure hunting on our own, without Mom or Dad. In fact, they were two of the treasures we'd recovered in our kids-only quests.

Now they were searching for buried treasure in the jungles of Cocos Island with just Tommy? Since when did the Kidd Family Treasure Hunters Inc. become a three-person operation instead of a six-person one?

Actually, it was dangerously close to becoming a four-person crew. Because the hungry hammerheads were much faster swimmers than me and Beck.

They were close and moving closer.

With a couple swift chomps of their jaws, they could definitely subtract two from six—permanently!

CHAPTER 2

I heard a rush of water behind me!

The hammerheads breathing down our butts had just thrown open their jaws. I could smell their stinky fish breath. I believe they had recently enjoyed the all-you-can-gobble shrimp buffet at the nearest coral-reef diner.

"So long, Beck!" I shouted, thrashing against the waves. "You're the best twin I ever had!"

"I'm the only twin you ever had!" she shouted back.

"This is no time to get all technical, Rebecca. We're both about to die!" As the storyteller of the family, I decided to wax poetic with my dying words. "I guess it's only fitting that since we came into this world together, we should leave it together, too!"

"Oh, no, you're not!" cried the heroic voice of our (you won't believe this) big sister, Storm!

She zoomed between us and the hammerheads on a Jet Ski!

"Where'd you find a Jet Ski?" I hollered.

"Tommy had it stowed in a secret compartment

in the bow of our ship!" Storm shouted back. "He might've forgotten that he told me about it, but I never did!"

The thing to remember about our big sister, Storm, is that she remembers everything. She's also the smartest Kidd kid. So why was she doing something as dumb as attempting to herd sharks on a Jet Ski? Because that's what we Kidds do. We look out for one another—even if we look ridiculous doing it.

"Whatever you do, Bick," Storm shouted, "don't pee! Sharks can smell human urine in the ocean."

Great, I thought. *Now she tells me.*

Storm circled the sharks, churning up a white, foamy wake to fence them in. More or less.

"Swim to shore, you two," she told us. "I'll keep these bad boys busy. I brought along one of Dad's golf clubs!"

As I frantically swam for the beach, I chanced a glance over my shoulder to see what Storm was doing with Dad's driver, the biggest club from his bag.

She jabbed at all of the sharks who dared snap at her as she zipped around and around them in dizzying circles. That's Shark-Attack Defense 101: Poke 'em in their gills.

Or their eyes!

"What are you looking at, M. C. Hammerhead?" Storm yelled at the lead shark.

One-handing the Jet Ski throttle, she used her free arm to line up the golf club's head with the shark's big, bulging eyeball as if it were sitting on a tee!

Storm faked like she was going to rear back with the driver. The alpha shark, who seemed dead set on eating us a moment earlier, turned tail and headed out to sea. Guess he didn't want to see one of his eyeballs ending up on the seventeenth green. It would make for a messy putt. The other sharks took off with him.

A couple minutes later, Beck and I dragged ourselves ashore. We were exhausted but alive, barely able to catch our breath.

Yay, Storm!

When she landed her Jet Ski on the beach and hauled it up on the sand, Beck and I raced down to give her a huge hug. We were both sooooo lucky to be part of the most incredibly awesome family in the world!

"Thank you, Storm!" said Beck.

"You're the best big sister we could ever have!" I added.

Storm didn't seem to be quite as happy as Beck and me.

I could see her eyes darken as she narrowed them at us.

Yep. That's why we call her Storm.

Like a thundercloud billowing up in the tropics, she can get very, very angry very, very quickly.

CHAPTER 3

"Mom and Dad told us to stay on board the *Lost*!" roared Storm. "It was a direct order. Stay on the ship, guard the Room."

"But we're treasure hunters!" I told her.

"So?"

"So we're this close to the legendary Treasure of Lima and we're supposed to just sit on the sidelines twiddling our thumbs while Mom, Dad, and Tommy have all the fun?"

"Yes," said Storm, who can be as blunt as a hammer even when she's nowhere near hammerhead sharks. She says exactly what she's thinking, no matter what.

"But Mom and Dad need us," said Beck.

"For what?"

"To help them figure out clues and junk!"

Storm raised a skeptical eyebrow. "Clues and junk?"

"You know," said Beck. "Stuff."

As you can probably tell, Beck's talents are more visual than verbal. (Fine. She says my BO is extremely visual, too—it's why she sometimes draws me with stink lines.)

"We have to help them," I pleaded. "This island is teeming with treasure!"

Even though I was pretty sure Storm had already memorized the whole entire history of Cocos Island, I launched into a swashbuckling tale of pirates and plunder from days past.

"For centuries," I proclaimed as dramatically as I could, "this island served as a buccaneers' bank! One daring pirate captain buried three hundred and fifty tons of gold he stole off Spanish royal galleons! His crew had to dig a really, really big hole!

"Then," I said, "there's the treasure Mom and Dad and Tommy think they've found." I took a long pause and sort of hoped there'd be an enormous thunderclap when I uttered my next words: "The long-lost Treasure of Lima!"

"Dun-dun-dun!" quipped Beck.

"We're talking a whole boatload of Incan gold and artifacts the Spaniards shipped from Peru to Mexico for safekeeping, way back in 1823.

WE STOLE ALL THIS GOLD FROM THE INCAS IN PERU! NOBODY BETTER TRY TO STEAL IT FROM US!

"But, arrr!" I said in my best talk-like-a-pirate voice. "The captain of that ship got greedy, me hearties. He went rogue and slit the throats of the guards traveling with the Incan gold. He threw the dead bodies overboard and brought the treasure here to Cocos, where he hid it high in the craggy hills! The captain and his scurvy mates planned on lying low, then coming back to retrieve their treasure. But they were captured and tried for piracy, and their buried booty has never been found!"

"I'm fully aware of the historical significance of this island," said Storm, who's usually the one giving the history lectures. "But the true moral of your pirate story is that when teams don't stick together and do what they're supposed to do, everybody loses!"

"That's exactly Bick's point!" said Beck.

"It is?"

Since I hadn't realized I'd been making a point, I couldn't wait to hear what Beck would say next!

CHAPTER 4

"Mom and Dad might need Bick and me," Beck told Storm, "to do our jobs on the team."

"Riiiiight," said Storm. "I almost forgot. You guys are in charge of junk and stuff."

"No. The team needs us for crawling in tight spaces."

"Huh?"

"Beck's right," I said. "She and I are the youngest and, therefore, the smallest and wiriest members of the family! Getting into tight spots is what we do best."

Storm rolled her eyes. "Tell me about it."

"It's like you said, Storm," added Beck. "If

we don't stick together, if everybody on our team doesn't do exactly what they're supposed to do, then we could lose the Treasure of Lima."

Storm exhaled. Loudly. "But you two were supposed to stay on board the *Lost* with me and guard the Room. That was our job!"

"Only because Mom and Dad forgot they might need us to crawl into a cave!" I told her. "If I were a pirate, that's where I would hide my treasure. Someplace so narrow, only someone our size could reach it."

"Then how'd the pirates get it in there in the first place?" demanded Storm, because, let's face it, she's way more logical than me.

"Cabin boys," said Beck.

"And monkeys," I added. "Pirates always have monkeys riding on their shoulders. Unless they go with parrots instead."

"Fine!" said Storm, sounding totally exasperated. "Whatever. Let's go find Mom and Dad and Tommy!"

She trudged up toward the jungle.

Beck and I high-fived. We'd totally double-teamed our big sister into submission. It's another twin thing.

Storm planned on using her photographic memory to lead us to the treasure site that Dad had pinpointed on a map in the Room. He had all sorts of rare maps in there. Some were so old, they even showed where you'd find sea serpents and other mysterious monsters.

One map—a recent discovery that Dad made in, believe it or not, Rome, Italy—might take us to the Lost City of Paititi deep in the Amazon rain forest. The map was an antique (dating all the way back to the 1600s) and cost Dad several hundred thousand dollars.

Legend says the Lost City of Paititi is filled with all the gold and precious gems that the last Incas of ancient Peru wanted to hide from the Spanish conquistadors looting their land.

"We have to hike up Mount Iglesias," announced Storm, gesturing to the leafy green peak in front of us.

"No problem," I said, even though I was huffing and puffing and sweating like I had a leaky bilge pump under each arm. (Look for Beck to start adding stink lines to my pits.)

"Um, how high is the summit?" asked Beck.

"Two thousand and seventy-nine feet," reported Storm.

"Oh," I said, as if it were no big deal. "At least it's not two thousand and eighty."

We had to cross a rickety bridge that park

rangers had made entirely out of gear confiscated from fishermen working illegally in the protected waters around Cocos Island. We knew

the backstory of the bridge because Tommy had, a day earlier, fallen hopelessly in love with one of the Costa Rican park rangers living on the island.

That's why Mom and Dad call our seventeen-year-old big brother "Tailspin" Tommy. Every time he sees a pretty girl, he nosedives hopelessly in love with her.

And sometimes, he takes the rest of us down with him!

CHAPTER 5

"Keep your eyes on the ground and always look ahead," said Storm, leading us deeper into the jungle, which was extremely hot and muggy.

That meant Beck, Storm, and I were extremely sweaty and grouchy.

Halfway up the slope of Mount Iglesias, trudging through the thick vines and drippy leaves, Beck and I erupted into one of our famous Twin Tirades. In case you're counting, this was number 1,103.

These flash rants are yet another twin thing. They're quick diatribes or outbursts of denunciation (words Mom put on our homeschool vocab quiz last week) that flare up like a match but burn out before the flame can scorch your fingertips. Beck and I get really, really angry with each other and then, usually in a minute or two, forget what we were angry about.

Storm was so used to our fast-moving squalls of fury that when this one blew through, she totally ignored it and kept hiking.

"When you think about it," I said, "I'm actually *the* most important member of the whole Kidd treasure-hunting team. I write up our adventures and share them with the world! If it weren't for me, no one would even know who we are."

"So? If it weren't for my drawings, nobody would even know *where* we are, pea brain."

"Yes, they would. I'd just write that we're on an island in the Pacific Ocean, three hundred and fifty miles off the coast of Costa Rica!"

"Says who?"

"Me!"

"Well, Bickford, a picture is worth a thousand words."

"That's a horrible cliché, Rebecca."

"So what? It's also true. See?"

ALOHA, EVERYBODY, WE'RE IN HAWAII!
WE'RE SUPPOSED TO BE OFF THE COAST OF COSTA RICA!
HAWAII IS OFF THE COAST OF COSTA RICA.
RIGHT. FIVE THOUSAND MILES OFF IT!
SO? WE'RE STILL IN THE PACIFIC OCEAN, AND YOUR PITS STILL SMELL WORSE THAN MOLDY PINEAPPLES MIXED WITH PICKLED PAPAYA!

"You can't draw us in Hawaii when we're in Central America!" I told her.

"Um, yes, I can, because I just did."

"Oh. So I guess your pictures are worth more than my words."

"Sometimes."

"That's very interesting, Beck."

"So are you, Bick."

"That's very benevolent of you to say, Beck."

"What's *benevolent* mean?"

"'Kind.'"

"Cool. Good word, Bick."

"Thanks."

"So, um, what were we arguing about?"

"I forget."

"Huh. Me, too."

And just like that, Twin Tirade number 1,103 was history.

We had hiked another twenty yards when, suddenly, Storm swung up her right arm to halt us in our tracks.

"What's wrong?" I asked.

"You two!" Storm replied in an angry whisper.

"All your shouting and Twin Tirade–ing may have attracted some unwanted attention."

"From who?" I whispered. "Tommy's girlfriend? Because park rangers are the island's only permanent residents."

"Incorrect, Bick."

Storm pointed off into the thick foliage.

All I could see were a bunch of green leaves, brown dirt, and a yellowish-brown lump of fuzzy black spots with bright yellow eyes.

The lump moved.

"Wh-wh-why is that cat wearing camouflage?" stammered Beck.

"Because," said Storm, "it is a jaguar, a name derived from the Tupian word *yaguara,* which means 'he who kills with one leap.'"

Storm.

I sometimes wish she wouldn't tell us *everything* she knows.

CHAPTER 6

"Back away slowly," coached Storm, who's memorized a ton of Jungle Survival Tips. "Avoid eye contact, which can be seen as a challenge."

The last thing I wanted to do was challenge one of the largest carnivorous cats in South America. The two-hundred-pound jaguar prowled forward on padded paws. The three of us backed up. Slowly. If you run away from any predator, it'll just think you're food. Fast food.

"Actually," said Storm, who is so filled with

facts they come spewing out exactly when you don't want to hear them, "you are more likely to be struck by lightning than attacked by a jaguar."

"Except," said Beck, "if there's one, like, ten yards away from you."

"True," said Storm. "If he lunges at you, be sure to cover your head with your hands."

"Why?" I asked.

"The jaguar is a unique hunter. Instead of biting you in the neck and going for your jugular, it sometimes sinks its teeth into the back of your head to pierce your brain."

Great, I thought. *Jaguars are like zombies. They want to eat braaaaains!*

We kept backing up, totally ignoring Storm's earlier instructions to keep our eyes on the ground and always look ahead.

Bad move.

Because we ended up blindly stepping back into a pit.

A snake pit!

"Ah," said Storm calmly, "that snake coiled

around that branch is the *Bothrops asper,* more commonly known as the fer-de-lance, or *terciopelo.*"

"Is it poisonous?" I gasped.

"Yes. Very. In fact, it's known as the ultimate pit viper due to its super-strong venom."

"But they only attack if attacked first, right?" said Beck as we all backed up to the other side of the pit, where the snake wasn't lurking.

Storm shook her head. "*Terciopelos* are

unpredictable. Here's another interesting factoid: a *terciopelo* can have sixty babies at once."

That made Beck and me hop up and down while we checked around our feet, searching for infant vipers. All I saw were some twigs and broken branches. No baby snakes. The super-viper giving us the beady eyeball from the other side of our mud hole was flying solo. That was a good thing. Then again, we still had that jaguar prowling around the rim of the pit to see if tonight's dinner would be marinated in juicy snake venom.

That's when the floor of the rain forest above our heads started squirming.

"Uh-oh," said Beck. "Looks like kindergarten's out for the day. Here come her babies!"

At least forty slimy little reptiles slithered up to the edge of our hole.

"Good-bye, Rebecca. Good-bye, Bickford," said Storm. "It has been an honor and a pleasure being your big sister. At least our deaths will be swift and this pit will serve as a convenient grave."

"Wait a second," I said. "Who says we're going to die?"

“Storm,” said Beck. “And all the itty-bitty baby snakes.”

“Who cares what they say? We’re the Kidds. We never give up without a fight.”

“This time,” said Storm, “perhaps we should. Did I mention that the fangs on a *terciopelo* are an inch long?”

“Then,” said Beck, “they might scare off a jaguar, too!”

“You thinking what I’m thinking?” I asked.

“Of course,” said Beck.

“It’s a twin thing,” we said together.

“Wait for it,” I said.

“Waiting,” said Beck.

The viper uncoiled herself from the tree limb and slithered down the far side of our pit.

“On three,” I said quickly.

Beck nodded.

“One...two...three!”

We each bent down as fast as we could and grabbed a stick with a forked end.

I jabbed my improvised tongs under Mama Snake’s head. Beck went for her midsection, maybe three feet down. With a grunt, we simultaneously heaved the snake up and away—sending her flying straight at the jaguar!

The baby snakes slithered off to find Mama. The jaguar took one look at the hissing snake's wide-open jaws and bolted.

Beck and I clambered out of the pit, reached down, and hauled Storm up.

Then the three of us went running up the trail—suspicious of every shadow and vine wiggling in the breeze.

CHAPTER 7

Finally, up ahead, near the summit of the mountain, we saw Mom, Dad, and Tommy.

They were standing outside a cave. Our awesome family was about to be reunited again—and none of us had been bitten by a poisonous snake or had our brains bashed in by a giant cat.

Mom saw us first. "Rebecca? Bickford? Stephanie?"

(Yep, Stephanie is Storm's real name. And Mom and Dad are the only ones allowed to use it.)

"What are you guys doing here?" asked Dad, who was holding some kind of golden crown topped with three gold-plated feathers.

"Chya," said Tommy. "What's up, dudes?" He held an ancient staff, also made of gold. It had a tomahawk-shaped head. He kept twisting the rod so he could check out his reflection in the flat part of the shiny golden blade.

“We thought you guys might need us,” I told Dad, who was giving us one of his very serious, pinched-eyebrow looks.

“We did need you,” said Dad. “To stay on board the ship and guard the *Lost*.”

“Don’t worry,” I said. “Beck made sure the Door was locked.”

“Um, actually,” Beck mumbled, “I thought *you* made sure it was locked.”

I guess that’s another twin thing: thinking your twin did the stuff you were supposed to do.

“Sooooo,” I said, hoping to change the subject, “did you guys find the long-lost Treasure of Lima?”

“Yes,” said Mom proudly. “And we’ve already hauled out the most important pieces.”

Luckily, they were so excited about the treasures that they didn’t give us any more grief about abandoning the ship. Not right then, anyway.

“That’s an ancient Incan priest’s headpiece,” said Tommy, gesturing at the glimmering crown Dad held in his hands.

“And,” said Mom, “Thomas is holding the high priest’s golden staff—a very powerful image in Incan mythology.”

“Check it out,” said Tommy. “There’s a golden ear of corn at the top!”

“And why is that?” asked Mom, who’s our homeschool history teacher on board the *Lost*.

Tommy got a pained expression on his face. It happens every time he tries to think. “Um, in case the priest wanted to make microwave popcorn?”

Mom laughed, shook her head, and turned to the smartest Kidd in our class. “Storm?”

“Maize, or corn, was the chief crop of the ancient Incas,” she answered. “Without it, their civilization would have vanished long before the Spanish conquistadors arrived in Peru.”

“Too bad there’s an empty hole at the top of the corncob,” said Tommy. “Probably where an oval-shaped emerald or ruby or something used to be. Guess it popped out on the boat ride up from Lima.”

It was pretty amazing to think that Dad and Tommy were holding relics from a long-lost

civilization. I could just picture the Inca high priest performing rituals with the gear. Fortunately, Beck could picture it even better!

CHAPTER 8

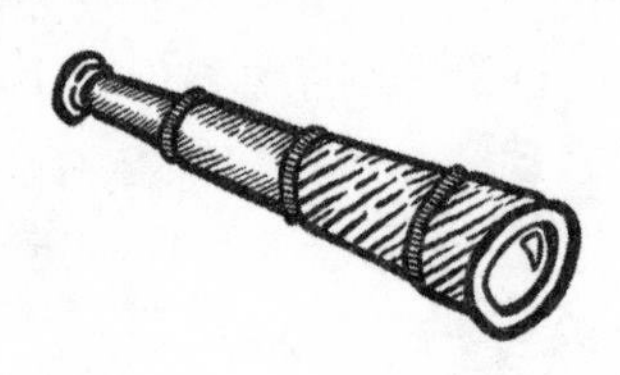

"We also found a very important document," said Dad, tapping his leather satchel. "A letter that might prove more valuable than the crown, the staff, or even the very curious artifact the letter was wrapped around."

"Why's the letter so important?" I asked.

"Because, Bick," said Dad with a wide smile, "it confirms that the Lost City of Paititi is more than just a legend."

"Paititi?" I said. "The Lost City of Gold?"

Mom nodded. "Hidden deep in the Amazon rain forest."

I turned to Dad. "You said there was an artifact inside the letter?"

"Indeed."

"Maybe they're connected!"

"Whoa," said Tommy. "I should've thought of that! Because the Incan head was like totally wrapped up inside the parchment the letter was written on."

Dad dipped into his shoulder bag and pulled out what looked to be a golden medallion carved to resemble an ancient Incan chief's head.

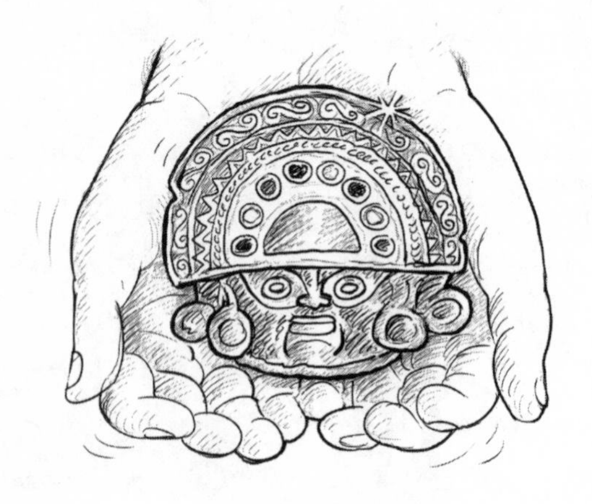

"What is it?" I asked. "I mean, besides an ancient gold emoji of a frowny face?"

"We're not certain," said Mom. "However, it might be the handle of an ancient Incan *tumi*."

"Is that Spanish for 'tummy'?" I asked.

"No," said Dad with a laugh. "A *tumi* is a ceremonial sacrificial knife, typically one with a very sharp, rounded blade at the bottom. The Incas used it at their annual harvest festivals to slay llamas—"

"And humans," blurted out Storm. "The Incas sacrificed humans, including children, to appease the sun god."

I told you—Storm has absolutely no filter between her brain and her mouth.

It was time to change the subject again. "So where's all the other gold?" I asked. "The coins and the statues and the jewels? All the stuff that was on that ship back in 1823?"

"Still in the cave," said Dad. "We don't have time to initiate a full recovery operation."

"What?" said Beck.

"We need to hurry to Peru," explained Mom. "The Lost City of Paititi is our primary goal. Treasure hunters have been searching for it for centuries."

"And now," said Dad, "we might finally have the tools to find it."

"B-b-but—" I said.

Dad cut me off midblubber.

"Now then," said Dad, tucking the *tumi*

fragment back into his bag, "as thrilled as we are with our finds, I must say, your mother and I are very disappointed in you three."

He was looking at Storm, Beck, and me.

"Storm only left the ship to save our lives," I said sheepishly.

"Whoa," said Tommy, sounding impressed. "Seriously?"

Storm nodded. "Swarm of hammerheads interested in a Bick-and-Beck sushi platter. I improvised a counterattack with your Jet Ski and Dad's golf clubs. Seemed to work."

"Awesome!"

Tommy and Storm exchanged high and low fives.

"Then we're not mad at you, Storm," said Mom. "But you two..."

"We're sorry," I said. "But come on. We're wild things. If there's a wild rumpus, we need to be there. We can't be cooped up on a ship when adventure calls!"

"Yo," said Tommy, "speaking of calls, did a

very attractive Costa Rican park ranger named Sileny happen to call while I was gone?"

"Who's Sileny?" asked Beck.

"The girl I'll probably marry one day. She's as beautiful as her name, which, by the way, means 'moonlight and silence.' Or maybe 'silent moonlight'..."

We all probably would've laughed at that except another roaring predator sprang out of the jungle.

This time it wasn't a jaguar.

This time it was worse!

CHAPTER 9

Six off-road dirt bikes, engines screaming and spewing smoke, thundered up the trail and surrounded us.

The helmeted riders skidded to a muddy stop and aimed their weapons at us!

When the leader of the pack took off his helmet to reveal a French Foreign Legion hat, I immediately recognized our old nemesis from our adventures in Egypt, Guy Dubonnet Merck! (His name rhymes with *I, how you say, jerk.*)

Not this guy again! (Ha, get it?)

YOU THOUGHT YOU COULD ESCAPE ME, FOOLISH KIDD CHILDREN? HA, I SAY. HA, HA, HA! WHY IS NO ONE ELSE LAUGHING?
DON'T LET IT HAPPEN AGAIN!
SORRY, BOSS. HA, HA. THAT IS SO FUNNY, WE FORGOT TO LAUGH.

"You guys?" said Dad. "Do you know this gentleman?"

"Chya," said Tommy.

I stepped forward and sort of sneered at the man with the eye patch. "That's Guy Dubonnet Merck."

"Ah, yes," said Mom. "Aunt Bela mentioned his name."

Aunt Bela had been Mom's handler when Mom worked with the CIA.

"He chased us around Africa when we were trying to rescue you and find Dad," added Beck.

"And then," said Storm with a grin, "we cleverly reduced him to a sniveling, blubbering lump of raggedy mosquito bites, which we left stranded near the entrance to King Solomon's Mines!"

"But I could find no mine!" snarled Merck. "No gold. No precious diamonds or jewels. You insolent brats tricked me!"

"Yes," said Storm. "We did. It was a beautiful thing."

"And, dude?" said Tommy. "You made it so totally easy. Next time, read a book, why don't you?"

"This *is* the next time, *mon ami,*" said Merck, pointing his pistol at Tommy.

"Whoa there," said Dad, raising his hand. "Take it easy, Mr. Merck."

"Take it easy? Ha, I say, Dr. Kidd. Ha!"

His five helmeted minions took their cue.

"Ha, ha, ha," they all said.

"Your vile children left me and my diseased feet to rot in the jungles of Africa!" screamed Merck.

Tommy turned to Mom and Dad. "You should've seen them. They were totally green and gnarly."

"Trench foot," I explained. "I had it, too."

"Silence!" shouted Merck.

Now all his henchmen racked their rifles.

"No more happy-family chitchat."

Dad made a finger tent under his nose and looked super-serious. "Was your family life happy when you were a child, Mr. Merck?"

(By the way, one of Dad's many degrees is in psychology.)

"Happy?" scoffed Merck. "Ha. We were

miserable. Miserable, I say! Every year for Christmas, all I ever got was a new shoelace for my eye patch!"

"And how did that make you feel?" asked Dad earnestly.

"Wretched! Horrible! Dirt-poor!" He paused. "But do not worry about me, Professor Kidd. I have found that which makes me happy!"

"And what is it?" said Mom. "What brings you joy, Mr. Merck?"

"Stealing shiny gold Incan antiques from foolish treasure hunters who allow their children to blab about what they are doing to everyone they meet! Especially if one of those new friends has a pretty face and a phony park ranger uniform!"

One of the bikers took off a helmet and shook out her hair.

Tommy gasped.

"Sileny?"

From the look on his face, Tommy was heartbroken. Again.

CHAPTER 10

Oh-kay. So much for Tommy's Costa Rican girlfriend's name meaning "silent."

I wonder what the Spanish word for "blabbermouth" is?

"Sileny?" Tommy sort of whimpered. "How could you?"

"Silence, silly boy!" hissed Sileny, reminding me of that pit viper we'd just met. "You were so easy to fool."

Tailspin Tommy crashes and burns once again.

Guy Dubonnet Merck chuckled.

"Give us the golden crown and the scepter of the Incan high priest, Dr. Kidd!" he demanded. "Give them to us now! Or I will execute your children one by one. Starting with the girl you call Storm, for she not only tricked me into a wild African goose chase, she is also a very easy and wide target."

Dad's face turned beet red. It always does when somebody makes fun of one of his children.

"I believe you meant to say she is beautiful and intelligent." I could see the hair bristling on the back of his neck.

"She will also be dead if you do not give me what I want!" raged Merck. "Do not forget, Dr. Kidd, I'm a semipsychotic sociopath compensating for a wretchedly unhappy childhood."

Whoa. I guess Guy Dubonnet Merck had a psych degree, too.

"Very well," said Dad. "If we give you the headpiece and the staff, do you promise you will leave my family unharmed?"

"Yes! You have my word as a semipsychotic sociopath!"

"Um, that's not the best vow I've ever heard," I said.

"Give them the golden rod, Tommy," said Dad.

"Fine," said Tommy. "But I'm not giving it to *her!*"

He handed the ancient Incan staff to the closest biker who wasn't Sileny.

"Here you are, Mr. Merck," said Dad, holding out the Incan headpiece. "I hope it brings you happiness and good fortune."

"Ha!" laughed Merck, grabbing the feathered crown out of Dad's hands. "I'm sure it will."

He cradled the headpiece in his lap so he could tap some information into his smartwatch.

He waited maybe five seconds.

His watch dinged.

"Voilà!" Merck announced. "I already have a buyer. Oh, my. Such a generous offer, too! *Adieu,* annoying Kidd family. It has been a pleasure robbing you. I would kill you all now but I hope to steal more treasures from you in the future. Sileny, my dove? Lead the way!"

The six dirt bikes took off, their spinning tires chewing up the jungle floor as they barreled down the trail.

"We should chase after them!" I said.

"An excellent suggestion, Bick," said Dad. "However, we forgot to pack our own trail bikes."

"I sure wish we had," said Beck.

"We still remember all those off-roading moves you taught us," I told Dad.

"I'm certain you do."

When Beck and I were younger, Dad spent a lot of time teaching us how to ride. We started on tricycles, of course, but we were driving ATVs on rugged mountain ranges all over the world when most kids our age were still on bikes with training wheels.

"We better get back to the ship," said Mom. "Fast."

"Indeed. But cheer up, family," said Dad. "All is not lost. Mr. Merck may have taken our shiny gold artifacts but he foolishly left us with the most important Incan treasures."

Dad tapped his shoulder bag again.

The letter and the handle of the sacrificial *tumi* knife were still in there. We still had the keys to the Lost City of Paititi.

"Let's double-time it down the mountain," said Mom.

"Yes, ma'am!" we all shouted back, including Dad. Then we took off jogging.

We could still hear the whine of the motorcycles

in the distance. It sounded like they were making their way to the other side of the island.

"Good," Dad said when we came to a cliff overlooking the bay where we had anchored the *Lost*. "Mr. Merck has no interest in looting our ship, too!"

"Chya," said Tommy, pulling out his binoculars and studying the sea below. "Maybe because somebody else already beat him to it!"

WHOEVER'S RAIDING OUR SHIP HAS A TOTALLY AWESOME-LOOKING MINI SUB.
GOOD THING YOU GUYS LOCKED THE DOOR TO THE ROOM.
SPLASH
OOPS.

CHAPTER 11

By the time we made it back to the *Lost,* the boarding party of pirates was gone.

So was the leather map Dad had discovered in Rome.

“The Door was unlocked?” said Mom, staring in disbelief at our wide-open bank vault. When she was done doing that, she stared at me and Beck. Hard.

“I thought Bick was going to check the lock,” said Beck.

“I thought Beck was going to do it,” I countered.

Beck whirled around to face me. “Well, then, you should’ve asked me if I was going to check the lock!”

“You could’ve asked me, too!”

We were about to erupt into our worst Twin Tirade ever when Storm spoke up.

“Guess it’s time for me to save your twin tushies again,” she said with a sigh. “Dad?”

“Yes?” he said. He sounded distracted, probably because we desperately needed that map to find Paititi.

“Don’t worry,” said Storm. She tapped her temple. “I memorized it.”

“What?” said Dad.

“The map. It was ink on leather. Full of interesting hieroglyphs.”

"When did you see it?"

"After I saw how important it was to you."

"But how did you get into the Room?" asked Mom.

"Easy. I memorized the code Dad punched into the security system the last time he locked it."

"Wait a second," I said to Storm. "So you're saying the Door wouldn't've been unlocked if you hadn't unlocked it?"

She just shrugged. "Guess not. But you should've checked. I can be forgetful about stuff like locking doors."

"What?" exclaimed Beck. "You have a photographic memory!"

"True. But I use it only for important information. Otherwise, my brain would become too crowded. Now, if you guys will excuse me, I'm going to go to my cabin, where I will re-create the map. I think I'll do it on my laptop instead of leather."

Storm eased past the rest of us and headed up to the cabin that she shared with Beck in the ship's bow.

Mom smiled. "We have an amazingly talented daughter, Thomas," she said to Dad.

"Indeed we do," said Dad.

"Bick and I could've chased after Merck," said Beck.

"If we'd had our trail bikes," I added.

"We know," said Dad. "You two are extremely talented, too."

"What about me?" Tommy moped. "What's my talent? Falling head over heels in love with girls who just want to steal our treasures?"

"You have a good heart, Tommy," said Mom.

"You're also an amazing big brother," said Beck.

"Totally," I chimed in. "We never would've survived without Mom and Dad if we didn't have you."

"Yeah, well, maybe. But this is it. I'm done. No more girlfriends. Well, at least not until I go to college. Or until next month. Maybe I'll just take a month off..."

"Sounds like a wise move, Tommy," said Dad. He checked his dive watch. "Time is of the essence,

Kidds. Whoever was on that submarine has our map and a head start."

"They're on their way to Paititi already!" I said, pounding my fist into my open palm.

"Perhaps," said Dad mysteriously. "However, the map may not help them all that much if they don't know how to decode it."

"And we do?"

Dad tapped his satchel again.

"Is that what's in the letter?" I asked.

"Yes, Bick. The letter is the true key to the Lost City of Gold! Without it, the map those submarine pirates stole is practically worthless."

CHAPTER 12

Dad told us more about the crinkly old parchment letter he'd found on Cocos Island.

"It was written by a priest named Father Toledo and addressed to 'His Holiness, the Pope.' The letter and the Incan artifact it was wrapped around were placed on board the same ship as the Treasure of Lima for the first leg of its journey to Rome."

"But the letter never made it past Costa Rica," said Mom.

"Because the captain went all pirate on everybody!" I said.

Dad nodded. "Not knowing he had in his hull a letter that might prove far more valuable than all the treasure he hoped to steal."

"Wait a second," said Tommy. "How come you found the leather map in Rome?"

"Because," explained Mom, "Father Toledo was a very clever man. He sent the map on one ship bound for Rome and the code for deciphering it on another!"

"That was wicked smart," said Tommy. "I never would've thought of it. I probably would've blabbed everything to the first pretty girl I met at the dock!"

Mom smiled. "Go easy on yourself, Tommy."

"So that's why the secret Incan City of Gold has never been found," I said. "The pope had the map to Paititi but not the magic map-decoder key!"

"Precisely," said Dad.

"So how did Father Toledo end up with a map to Paititi?" I asked.

"By befriending a local. He used his medical knowledge to save the life of a man's young daughter. In gratitude, the local told the priest where he could find the fabled City of Gold."

"So, was everything in this Incan City of Gold made out of, you know, gold? Like, even the street lamps and sewer pipes and junk?" asked Tommy.

MOST EXPENSIVE FIRE HYDRANTS IN ALL OF SOUTH AMERICA!

"Were the streets paved with gold bars instead of bricks?" asked Beck.

"Not exactly, you guys," said Mom. Then, while we packed up our gear for the trip south, she gave us a quick refresher course on Paititi.

"According to legends, the city of Paititi was built by the Incan hero Inkarri, who had outfoxed the Spanish conquistadors and slipped away with more than twenty thousand llamas loaded down with gold and silver!"

“So, once Storm re-creates the map,” I said, “we can use Father Toledo’s letter to find where Inkarri stashed all that gold and silver!”

“Not right away,” said Dad. “First we must find the Sacred Stone.”

“Um, why?” asked Tommy.

“Because,” said Dad, reading and translating from the parchment letter, “according to Father Toledo, ‘One must first possess the Sacred Stone or the gates to Paititi will remain forever locked!’”

CHAPTER 13

"This is, like, the most complicated treasure hunt ever," I complained to Beck when we were up on deck at sunset, packing gear into duffel bags for the excursion into the Amazon rain forest.

"Totally," she agreed.

Yep, instead of a Twin Tirade, we were having a Twin Harmonious Convergence, a very rare event during which we both peacefully agree about everything. This was only number seven of those.

"First Dad had to find a map in Rome," said Beck.

"Then," I continued, "we had to dig up a Dear Pope letter off the coast of Costa Rica."

"Next," said Beck, "we have to find the Sacred Stone. What comes after that? The magical marimba? The enchanted empanada?"

"And this very minute, the rest of the Treasure of Lima is sitting right over there," I said, gesturing toward Cocos Island, since we were still anchored in its bay. "We just have to crawl into the cave and take it."

"So why don't we?" said Beck.

"Let's do it."

"I agree."

"Wow," I said. "These Twin Harmonious Convergences are even shorter than Twin Tirades."

"There's less spit involved, too."

"We should take a vote," I suggested. "See if Storm and Tommy agree with us."

"Good idea."

We bustled down belowdecks to see what

Storm thought. She'd just finished the treasure map she'd created from memory and was printing it out.

"I'm with you guys," she said after we told her our idea about going back to Cocos even though Mom and Dad said we didn't have time. "This map is so convoluted and confusing, it might just be one piece of a bigger puzzle. We could end up spending years hiking around in the rain forest. And I hate humidity."

Next we polled Tommy.

"We should definitely go back," he said. "Merck and Sileny saw us outside that cave. They might put two and two together and decide to go back to steal some more treasure from us."

Long story short, the four of us went to Mom and Dad and presented our arguments for going back to the island to retrieve the rest of the treasure.

"We should take a family vote!" I said.

"Fine," said Dad.

So we did.

It was four against two. Me, Beck, Storm, and Tommy against Mom and Dad.

But that didn't mean we won.

"I'm sorry, guys," said Dad with a heavy sigh. "Mom and I have to veto your vote. We are not going back to the island. Too much is at stake."

"Now go to bed," said Mom. "It's getting late. We're heading to Peru first thing tomorrow morning."

CHAPTER 14

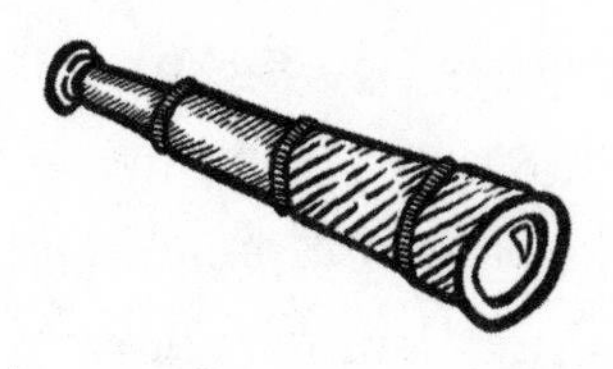

There was a whole lot of grousing and grumbling belowdecks that evening.

The four of us gathered in the cabin Tommy and I shared in the bow of our ship. We were all keeping our voices down because Mom and Dad were only two cabins away, snoozing peacefully. Well, we knew Dad was. We could hear his snoring. It sounded like a bear with breathing problems sawing a stump.

None of us could figure out how Mom could sleep next to that much noise. Maybe when she was a baby, she had a teddy bear that snored, too.

"Remember the good old days?" I whispered. "Like, a few months ago? When Mom was kidnapped and you guys all thought Dad was dead?"

Storm raised her eyebrows. "And those days were good *how*, exactly?"

"Not the stuff about Mom and Dad," I answered quickly. "Missing them was horrible."

"Scary, too," added Beck.

"Definitely," I said. "But back then, when we decided to do something, we did it!"

"Chya," said Tommy. "I'm kind of surprised we're all still alive. Remember when your feet nearly rotted off in Africa, Bick?"

"Yes, Tommy. Thanks for reminding me."

"No problemo, little bro."

"Now it's as if our votes don't count," said Beck. "Four against two and we lose? The system is rigged."

"Actually," said Tommy, "I think parental units always get three votes each. It's like a rule or something."

"Well, it's a bad rule!" I said.

We debated the issue for maybe fifteen more

minutes. Tommy kept reminding us of all the gross stuff that happened on our kids-only Kidd adventures.

Finally, we took another vote.

"Who wants to go back to the island tonight and haul all that treasure out of the cave?" I asked.

Four hands went up again.

"Then let's do it!" said Beck.

CHAPTER 15

We tiptoed up the hall, past the engine room, past Mom and Dad's room, where the snoring inside must have been rattling some of the tribal masks and priceless artifacts mounted on the walls.

We quietly made our way through the whitewashed galley and up the creaky wooden stairs to the deck.

Finally, we reached the rubber raft we used to travel ashore.

Mom was there, waiting for us.

“Hi, guys,” she said super-calmly. “Did you want to borrow the boat?”

“Um, sort of,” said Tommy.

“Still thinking about heading back to Cocos Island to pick up all that treasure we left behind?”

The four of us nodded because none of us can ever lie to our mother.

"Very well," she said, stepping out of the landing craft. "You have a choice. You guys can take this boat and go off on your own, or you can trust that your dad and I might know what's best—not just for this family but for a whole bunch of other people, too."

"Who?" I asked.

"The people of Peru. Don't forget, all that gold was stolen from them centuries ago. Your father and I made some discreet calls through back channels. Our good friend Dr. Maria Solis, a Peruvian anthropologist and archaeologist from the National University of San Marcos, is heading up an expedition that will initiate the recovery on Cocos."

"Oh," I said.

"So we're not just leaving it there sitting in a hole?" said Beck.

Mom smiled. "Nope."

"Cool," said Tommy with a yawn. "Let's skip the island and go to Peru tomorrow. Catch you guys later. I'm sleepy."

"Yeah," said Storm. "Me, too."

"Night, Mom," I said.

"See you in the morning," added Beck.

And together we headed back downstairs, trusting that Mom and Dad probably knew what was best.

That's why they got all those extra votes.

CHAPTER 16

The next morning, Tommy and I were both rudely awakened by the roar of airplane engines.

The snarling grew closer and was followed by a very loud, very long splash.

It sounded like somebody had just sent a school bus down a waterslide.

The *Lost* rocked as the wake of whatever had just sliced through the Pacific Ocean washed up against its hull.

"What the heck was that?" I said, bolting up in my bed and hitting the hardwood ceiling. Yes, Tommy always calls dibs on the lower bunk.

"Might be Dad's new toy," said Tommy.

"Huh?"

"You didn't think we were going to sail the *Lost* all the way to Peru, did you? Especially not if we want to beat those submarine pirates who stole the map to Paititi."

"Well, how else are we gonna get there?"

Tommy went to the porthole.

"Check it out. The Kidd Family Treasure Hunters' newest piece of exploration gear. A fully loaded and customized Seastar amphibious flying boat!"

A smiling guy was standing on one of the amphibious aircraft's wings, waving at me and Tommy.

"Um, is that our pilot?"

"Nah. Mom and Dad both have licenses. They'll handle the flying. That's just George."

"George?"

"He used to work with Mom and Dad at..." Tommy lowered his voice. "The Agency."

"He's from the CIA? George's a spy?"

"Shhh," said Tommy. "We're not supposed to use the S word, remember? George will guard the *Lost* while we're in Peru."

"Can we trust him?" I asked.

"Totally. Don't forget, he's an S word."

"So was strange Uncle Timothy!"

"True," said Tommy. "But George's not wearing mirrored sunglasses like Uncle T always did."

I nodded like that made sense because it sort of did.

"Come on," said Tommy. "We need to hustle."

CHAPTER 17

Tommy and I hauled our personal duffels up to the deck.

Storm and Beck were already there. Mom and Dad, too.

George tossed us a line so we could dock the seaplane right next to the *Lost.* He climbed up onto the deck and saluted Mom and Dad.

"The cow is in the barn," he said.

Dad nodded.

"The walrus sleeps in the sun," said Dad.

George nodded.

"The sparrows are ready to take flight," added Mom.

George and Dad nodded.

Yep, all the spies and former spies knew what they were saying. Us kids? We had nothing.

"Don't worry about your ship, Thomas," George said to Dad. "I'll keep an eye on it. So will our CIA satellites."

"Appreciate it. You know how to reach us?"

"Affirmative." He turned to Mom. "When's the big confab, Sue?"

"Soon. I'm waiting for the call. So are our activist allies in the rain forest. Hopefully, we'll have the rest of the money lined up before the Peruvian president calls all the parties to the table."

"What's your opening bid?"

"We're hoping to double whatever the loggers offer," said Mom.

"Impressive," said George.

"If we find the Lost City of Paititi," said Dad, "we might be able to quadruple what the lumber boys are willing to pay. We can save several million acres of rain forest from destruction."

Beck and I looked at each other.

It was our turn to nod. Finally, we knew exactly what Mom and Dad were up to.

We weren't just going to recover the extremely valuable relics of a long-lost civilization. Nope. As always, Mom and Dad were more interested in saving the most valuable treasure on Earth: Earth itself!

CHAPTER 18

Gear loaded and seat belts secured, we zoomed across the rippling waves.

The huge plane gained speed and gently lifted off the ocean like a Costa Rican pelican heading out on a fishing expedition.

"We'll call this amphibious aircraft the *Platypus*!" said Dad.

"And why is that a good name?" Mom asked over her shoulder from the copilot seat.

"Because," said Beck, "the platypus is a semiaquatic amphibious mammal."

"Just like us!" I added. "We're good on land or in the sea."

Everybody laughed.

By the way, flying in an amphibious aircraft is totally awesome. Especially one with comfy leather seats, computer monitors, and a galley stocked with Peruvian snacks and drinks. Mom called the choice of snacks "cultural immersion."

I called it chowing down on roasted salted corn, deep-fried cinnamon-dusted churros stuffed with vanilla cream, and bags of *chifles,* which, by the way, are banana chips. Delish. We washed it all down with Incan Kola, *el sabor del Perú* ("the flavor of Peru"), which is bright yellow, very sweet, and tastes like lemon-flavored bubble gum.

Dad manned the controls and Mom swiveled around in her copilot seat to give us a "quick history lesson" about the Lost City of Paititi legend.

(I guess that's the major problem with being homeschooled. Class time can be any time.)

"In the Quechuan language," said Mom, "Paititi means 'Home of the Jaguar Father.'"

Tommy raised his hand. "Does the big cat still live there?"

"Doubtful. The legendary city is believed to be hidden in the remote rain forests of southeastern Peru, east of the Andes. The descendants of the Incas, the Quechuans, tell stories of how their hero Inkarri saved a mountain of gold, silver, and sacred jewels from the Spanish conquistadors by fleeing into the jungle and establishing his hidden city behind the towering mountains."

"There are other legends," said Storm, who usually acts as Mom's teaching assistant. "One tells of a magnificent Incan gold chain, six hundred and fifty feet long, with links as thick as a thumb. Another speaks of a huge golden disk, thirteen feet wide."

"Whoa," said Tommy. "The whole disk was made out of gold?"

"Completely," said Storm. "The Incas used it in sacred sun-worshipping ceremonies."

"If it's solid gold, it would make an awesome sun reflector," said Tommy. "I bet you could get an incredible tan sitting in the center of it!"

WHAT? DO YOU THINK THE NECKLACE IS TOO MUCH? IS IT GIVING ME A TAN LINE?

"You wouldn't want to sit in the middle of the Punchao, Tommy," said Storm. "It was considered holy. Plus, the Incas sometimes used the big sacred object as an altar for sacrifices. *Human* sacrifices."

"You mean *human* as in people?"

Storm nodded. "Including children. And teenagers."

"Gotcha," said Tommy. "Good to know."

"And then," said Mom, "there's the most horrible legend of them all."

"Worse than Tommy's sunbathing story?" said Beck. "No way."

"Oh, it's much worse. This story is about what happened to Inkarri!"

CHAPTER 19

"Actually," said Storm, because she's always the smartest kid in the class even when the class is ten thousand feet above sea level, "Inkarri is a phonetic Quechua version of the Spanish words Inca and *rey*."

"That means 'Incan king'!" said Beck, who'd already done the Spanish homework I probably should've done, too.

"Exactly," said Mom. "The last king of the Incas, Inkarri, might have saved a lot of his people's treasure from the Spaniards but he couldn't save his own life."

"They chopped off his head," said Storm. She

even gave us the ol' finger-across-the-throat gesture with full *sniiiick* sound effects. Yeah. She can get gruesome. It's one of the reasons we love her.

"Worse," said Mom. "Inkarri's head was buried in one place while the rest of his body was buried someplace else."

"Or," added Storm, "some *places* else. A leg here, an arm there, another leg there—"

"Okay, okay," said Tommy. "We get the picture."

"And it is an extremely grisly picture that you paint," said Dad from the pilot's seat.

Guess Storm's grisly description was kind of grossing him out, too.

"In all Inkarri legends," said Mom, "the final Incan king vows to avenge his death and the mistreatment of the Peruvian people. When his head and body parts are reunited, it will mean the end of the darkness and despair brought to the Incas by the Spanish conquest. When Inkarri is restored, he will rise up from the earth. The Andean people will likewise rise up to reclaim what is rightfully theirs!"

"You think, when he pulls himself together, Inkarri will want his gold back?" asked Tommy.

"I would," said Beck.

I agreed. "Me, too. Paititi is like his piggy bank."

"Except, unlike yours," said Beck, "his has some coins inside it."

"And a big gold chain," added Tommy.

"And jewels," said Beck.

"And silver," I said. "And more gold..."

Mom laughed. "All those riches are why so many treasure hunters have spent so many years searching for the hidden city."

"Many have even lost their lives in their quest for the Lost City of Gold!" said Storm, who was totally in a gross-out-the-sibs mood.

"But we've got the map!" I said. "And the letter explaining how to read the map. So we'll be fine. Right?"

"Of course," said Dad, pushing his control wheel forward. "First stop, the Port of Pisco, one hundred and twenty-seven miles south of Lima."

"We're going to Pisco because there was a bird near a body of water on the leather treasure map!" exclaimed Storm.

"Well done, Storm!" said Dad. "An excellent display of your mastery of cartography as well as your comprehension of the Quechuan language!"

"Huh?" I said, and from the look on Tommy's and Beck's faces, I could tell they were thinking the same thing.

CHAPTER 20

"Cartography is the study and practice of map-making," said Mom, swiveling her copilot seat back around to the front so she could assist Dad in our approach and landing in Pisco.

"And," said Storm, "*pisco* is the Quechua word for 'bird'!"

She tapped the screen of her laptop, where our glowing treasure map was displayed. Our dotted-line journey started at a pelican perched on the coast of a rippling body of water with no edge.

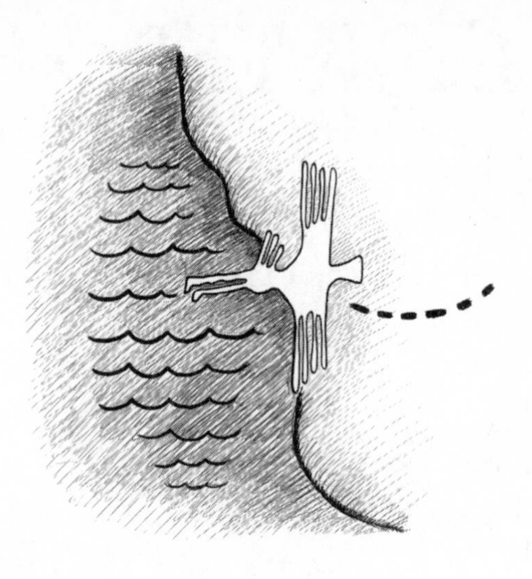

The water was, obviously, the Pacific Ocean. The bird had to be the port city of Pisco. Duh. It all made sense. After, you know, you studied and understood junk.

"A treasure map is impossible to follow," said Dad from the pilot seat, "unless you know exactly where to start your trek. Buckle up, everybody. We are beginning our initial descent into the Port of Pisco."

"Taking us to five thousand feet," said Mom, twisting dials on the cockpit instruments.

"Five thousand," said Dad, reading the altimeter. "Take us down to three."

"Three thousand."

While Mom and Dad continued taking us lower and lower, I looked out the window. All I saw was the Pacific Ocean, a bunch of tiny islands, and all sorts of birds.

"Um, Mom and Dad?" I said. "I don't see a runway."

Dad laughed. "We don't need one, Bick. This is a seaplane, remember?"

"Oh. Right. My bad."

"*They* don't need a runway either!" said Tommy, sounding mad. He was peering out the windows on his side of the plane.

"What's wrong, Thomas?" asked Mom.

"It's them! The pirates who stole our leather treasure map. I'd recognize their submarine anywhere!"

LOOK! A PELICAN!
JUST LIKE ON THE LEATHER MAP!
THIS MUST BE THE PLACE!
LET'S GO BUST OPEN INKARRI'S PIGGY BANK!

CHAPTER 21

"I suppose even a gang of imbecilic pirates could decipher the first point on the treasure map," said Dad, tilting his control wheel forward, sending us into a pretty steep dive. "Let's go pay those pirates a little visit!"

All those Peruvian snacks I'd been munching on? They were dancing the *pukllay* in my stomach (that's a carnival dance widespread among Peruvians that Mom made us learn in homeschool gym class). I was afraid that if we kept nosediving toward the ocean, those same snacks might lurch up into my mouth to dance the *puke*-lay!

"We're descending too rapidly, Thomas. I don't want them to get away."

Suddenly, Tommy was unbuckling his seat belt. "How low can you level off at?" he asked.

"Why?" asked Dad.

"I'll hop out and have a quick word with the pirates!"

"Thomas?" said Mom. "Sit down this instant."

"I can't," said Tommy. "I ripped off my seat cushion so I could use it as a flotation device."

"Thomas?" said Mom. "This isn't safe!"

"Sue, you heard the boy. Tommy doesn't have a seat to sit in! Nothing's more unsafe than that! Descend to ten meters. Thirty-three feet."

"The official height of an Olympic diving platform," said Storm.

"Hurry, you guys!" said Tommy, yanking open a door on his side of the plane.

A bag of churros went flying out.

"The first guy's already down the hatch and in the submarine!"

"Just ID them, son," advised Dad. "Don't try anything heroic or stupid."

"Of course not!"

And then Tommy immediately did something

I thought was kind of heroic *and* stupid.

He leaped out of our roaring seaplane!

CHAPTER 22

Dad banked the plane into a sharp, stomach-churning 180-degree turn so we could swing back and land in the ocean, right next to where Tommy dove in. Beck and I called the play-by-play from windows on opposite sides of the plane. Storm was busy with a barf bag. She'd wolfed down a couple churros, too.

"The sub is going under!" I announced.

"They're getting away!" added Beck.

"Tommy's fine," I said.

"Floating on his seat cushion."

The plane's pontoons touched down and sliced through the waves.

“Reverse thrust,” said Dad.

“Reversing,” said Mom.

And then they both said a bunch more pilot stuff until the seaplane puttered to a stop right next to our bobbing brother.

I tossed a line out the open door.

“You okay, Tommy?”

“Yeah,” he said, catching the rope and pulling himself over to the plane. “But there was no way to ID them. It’s an unmarked submarine.”

Storm looked up from her paper puke bag. “They’re pirates. It’s what they do.”

Beck and I helped Tommy haul himself back into the plane.

“Sorry about the seat cushion,” he said to Mom. “I think I trashed it. It’s soaking wet.”

Mom smiled. “So are you.”

“Chya,” said Tommy with a grin.

And that’s when a mysterious dugout canoe paddled up alongside our seaplane.

CHAPTER 23

A boy, younger than me, was manning the oar. A guy, probably in his twenties, decked out in full safari gear with a video camera propped on his shoulder, was perched up in the bow.

"Bravo, Tommy!" said the guy with the camera. "Awesome action sequence, man! Got it all on tape. We'll use it in the first episode, fer shure."

"Who the heck are you?" Beck shouted out our open seaplane door. "And how did you know Tommy's name?"

"Indeed," said Dad. "I was about to ask the same two questions."

While Dad was smiling out the window at our visitors to his left, his right hand was slowly snapping open a secret compartment in the cockpit floor.

I'm guessing that's where he'd asked George the spy to stow some kind of defensive weapon in case we encountered hostilities on our hop down to Peru. Dad's big on hiding stuff in strange places on board all our planes, boats, and motorized vehicles. The main mast on the *Lost*? These days, that's where Dad hides his antique jousting lance—just in case.

"I'm a really big fan," said the camera guy, bobbing up and down in the bow of the canoe. "Big, big fan. I know all about you Kidds and your treasure-hunting adventures, because I work for my father's most popular TV show."

He ran a hand across the sky like he was

reading a billboard and said: *"Nathan Collier's Treasure Trove of Treasure-Hunting Treasure Hunters."* This big hocking class ring he was wearing sparkled in the sun.

It was a horrible title for a TV show. Not just because it repeated itself. Nope. What made it super-stinky was the first part: *Nathan Collier!*

Tommy angrily narrowed his eyes. "Collier." He choked out the word, especially that *K* sound.

"That's right. I'm his oldest son, Chet Collier."

"Collier," Tommy said again. This time, he spat out the *K*.

"Whoa!" said Chet. "Ease up, dude. I know you guys and my dad have had your differences in the past."

"That, my friend," said our father, "would be an understatement."

For years, Nathan Collier has been our mom and dad's number-one nemesis. Their supervillain archrival. Collier is another treasure hunter who is forever trying to snatch their finds out from under them or take credit for their discoveries because he isn't very good at bringing anything up from a dive besides kelp-covered rubber boots. But Collier looks good on TV—with a slick smile and even slicker hair.

Nathan Collier hosted a whole bunch of shows on something called the Adventure Channel. It's one of the lesser-known cable networks. Right up there with the Watching-Paint-Dry Channel.

"Dad's turned over a new leaf," said Chet Collier.

"Why?" snarled Tommy. "Did he see somebody else under a palm tree turning over leaves and decide to steal their idea?"

"It's just an expression, dude. Means he's changed. He's not the creepy sleezoid I knew when I was young. He's mellowed, man. Thinks you Kidds are the world's greatest treasure hunters."

"Is that so?" muttered Dad skeptically.

"Totally!" said Chet. "That's why he sent me here to produce our brand-new TV special: *The Kidd Family Treasure Hunters*!"

"Wait a second," said Tommy, his snarl relaxing into something resembling a quizzical smile. "You want to turn us into TV stars?"

"Exactly. And Tommy?"

"Yeah?"

"Just between you and me, bro? Chicks dig TV stars!"

CHAPTER 24

"Look," said Chet Collier, still bobbing up and down in the canoe, "Dad knows he can never be as good as the Kidd family."

"It's true," said Storm. "And I have the statistics to back that up."

"I'm sure you do, Stormy."

"*Storm*. There is no *ee* sound at the end. Ever."

"Gotcha," said Chet. He tapped his temple. "Making a mental note. I'll tell the writers we have scripting your reality show."

"Reality show?" said Beck.

"That's right. We follow the Kidd Family Treasure Hunters in action, here in Peru or wherever else you guys want to go exploring. You'll be like the Von Trapp family in *The Sound of Music,* but without the singing. Love to talk to you folks about it, give you the pitch. Someplace where I'm not bobbing up and down so much."

Dad and Mom agreed to "hear what young Mr. Collier has to say."

We docked the seaplane with a local named Jorge who wore silver aviator sunglasses and somehow reminded me of George the CIA guy.

"El pastor cuida de sus oveja," said Jorge as he and Dad shook hands.

"Eso no es una oveja," said Dad. *"Es un hidroavión."*

I had no idea what they were saying. Guess I really should've done my Spanish homework.

Storm understood everything, of course. Guess that's why she was giggling. (Storm eventually told me it was spy mumbo jumbo, except the code words were in Spanish. Something about sheep.)

Anyway, Chet Collier took us to a seaside café with a sign in English advertising FRESH FISH.

I just hoped his pitch didn't stink as bad as yesterday's needlefish sitting in the sun.

FRESH FISH
HEY, BECK, WHY DID THE OCTOPUS CROSS THE ROAD?
I DUNNO, WHY?
TO GET TO THE OTHER TIDE.
SLURP

"Let me put this on the deck and see if you folks swab it up," said Chet. He nervously fidgeted with the ring on his finger while he made his pitch. "Me and my camera follow the six of you on your current treasure-hunting adventure. I get all sorts of amazing footage—you trekking through the jungle, crossing the Andes, deciphering ancient treasure maps, digging up priceless relics. Then we mix in the family element: Mom and Dad. Sons and daughters. The laughter and the tears. The high jinks and the highly emotional moments when you wonder if you're on this journey for the right reasons. You guys just being, well, you."

"Seriously?" said Beck. "You want to film Bick being Bick? Have you ever been downwind of him? They eat a lot of beans in Peru, right?"

"I want the good, the bad, and the stinky!" said Chet. "And Tommy?"

"Chya?"

"I want to turn you into the world's next teenage heartthrob!"

CHAPTER 25

"I'm in!" said Tommy. "Should I walk around without a shirt a lot?"

"Probably not a great idea, son," said Dad. "We'll be heading into the rain forest on this quest."

"There are mosquitoes in the rain forest," added Mom. "Big ones."

"Not to mention brown recluse spiders," said Storm.

"Are they poisonous?" asked Tommy.

"Very. Their venom is hemotoxic."

"Um, what does that mean?" I asked.

"It can cause necrosis of the skin," said Storm.

"And what does *that* mean?" asked Beck. "No big doctor words allowed."

"Fine," said Storm. "It means that your skin will die and melt away."

"Oh-kay," said Tommy, turning to Chet. "The shirt stays on. I might wear gloves, too."

"No problem," said Chet. "How about the rest of you Kidds? Are you in? Can I turn you all into TV stars?"

Mom and Dad stroked their chins and looked at each other.

While they were mulling it over, I jumped in with a quick question.

"So how'd you even know we were coming to Peru?" I asked.

Chet winked. "We work for a basic-cable network. We know all sorts of stuff."

"Well," said Beck, tag-teaming him with me (it's another twin thing), "how do we know your father's really changed his ways? The last time we dealt with him and his knuckle-dragging goons, they were trying to steal a Grecian urn from us in New York City."

Chet smiled. “Dad figured you might still be upset about that.”

“Well, duh!” Beck and I said together.

“So he made this video message.”

Chet pulled out his phone and played us a clip of his father apologizing. Profusely.

“I’m so, so sorry!” said Nathan Collier on the small screen. He was in a TV studio somewhere, standing in front of a giant logo for the Adventure Channel.

"I'm sorry I ever kidnapped any of you," Collier said on the screen. "I'm also extremely sorry that I had my Ukrainian henchpeople threaten you with their nasty rifles and that I had some other henchpeople steal that piece of pottery you kids needed to ransom your mother. I want you all to know that I have fired all of my minions, cronies, and lackeys. I promise: no more henchpeople. Please forgive me? If you do, I promise that my son and I will turn you and the noble causes you care so much about into TV sensations."

After he said that last bit, Mom nodded at Dad.

"This kind of coverage would definitely help us make our case to the Peruvian president," said Mom. "We can record up-to-the-minute evidence of the rain-forest deforestation and take the video with us to the big meeting."

"Whatever you need, Mrs. Kidd," said Chet.

"Very well," said Dad. "It's decided. Mr. Collier? Pack up your gear. You're coming with us."

Beck and I looked at each other and shook our heads.

We couldn't believe what was going on.

Now Mom and Dad didn't need their extra parental votes to overrule us kids because we weren't even taking family votes anymore.

This had become a Mom-and-Dad dictatorship.

CHAPTER 26

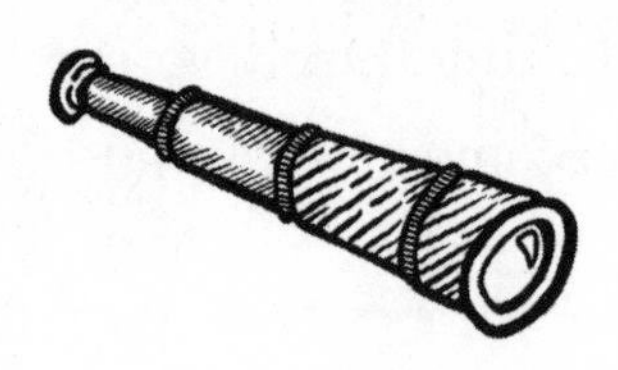

Our waiter brought us steaming plates of seafood pasta, so Beck and I decided to let off a little steam.

We put a new spin on our Twin Tirades. Instead of taking each other on, we turned on Mom and Dad, who, by the way, decided to label this kind of outburst, if it ever happened again, a Twin Tantrum.

"This is so unfair," said Beck.

"It is *egregiously* unfair!" I added.

"You guys aren't the boss of us!" said Beck.

"Well, technically, you are until we turn eighteen," I said. "Unless we're in Denmark, then it would be sixteen. Same in Liechtenstein."

"But that's not the point!" said Beck.

"No," I said, "the point is, you weren't with us when Nathan Collier was doing all that nefarious, despicable, and malicious stuff while we were busy trying to rescue you guys!"

"He was also evil," added Beck.

"That's what all those words I just used mean," I told her.

"Then why didn't you just say *evil?*"

"Because I'm a writer!"

"No, you're a wronger."

Yep. Our Twin Tantrum had morphed back into a Twin Tirade (number 1,104, if you're keeping score at home).

"*Wronger* isn't even a word," I shouted at Beck. "You'd have to say *more wrong.*"

"Fine. Bick, you're a more wrong."

"Oooh. That doesn't sound nice."

"You're right. Sorry."

"No worries."

"It'll never happen again."

"Great."

"So we're cool?"

"Totally."

Chet Collier was gawking at us. Understandable. He'd never witnessed the fast-moving fury of a Twin Tirade or a Twin Tantrum. Storm and Tommy, however, were rolling their eyes at us. They'd seen too many of our eruptions. Like, 1,103 too many.

Mom and Dad shook their heads and laughed.

"How about us?" asked Dad. "Are we cool, too?"

Beck and I both gave him a look like we were willing to think about it.

"You guys," said Mom, "having Mr. Collier and his camera recording whatever we discover will help us achieve our ultimate goals: Doing what is best for the people of Peru. And helping to save the planet."

"Turning me into an international superstar," added Tommy.

Beck and I sighed simultaneously.

"Fine," I said. "Mr. Collier can come with us."

"Awesome!" said Chet. "Where to first?"

Dad turned to Storm.

"We have a ways to go until we reach the Andes Mountains and then the rain forest," she said, prying open her laptop. She tapped a couple keys and called up her map app.

Chet tried to peek at it.

Storm slammed the lid shut.

"You don't need to see the map," she told Collier. "You just need to follow us with your camera."

"Riiiight," said Chet.

"We need to go to Cuzco," Storm announced. "The historic capital of the ancient Incan Empire."

"Cool," said Chet. "Was Cuzco on the map?"

"No," said Storm. "This is a treasure map. It doesn't spell things out for you, Mr. Collier, it makes you use your brain. Otherwise, anybody could find the treasure. Including your father!"

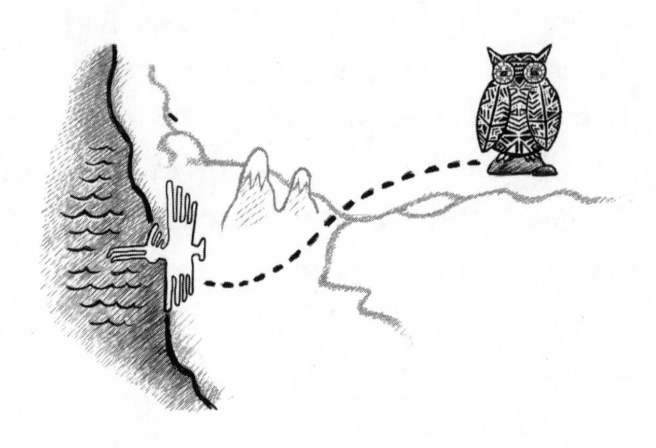

"Remind me, Storm," said Dad. "What were the graphics that helped you decipher Cuzco?"

"An owl perched on a rock."

"Well done!" said Dad, pulling out his high-tech satellite phone. "I'll contact Jorge. Ask him to prep the *Platypus*. We need to fly to Cuzco!"

CHAPTER 27

Mom and Dad charted a course from Pisco Bay to Cuzco, a city in southeastern Peru near a valley in the Andes Mountains.

"How'd you know we're supposed to go to Cuzco next?" I asked Storm once the *Platypus* was airborne.

"Yeah," said Chet Collier. "How'd you know?"

Collier was strapped in between me and Beck on the rear bench seat. The three of us were facing Storm and Tommy (who was trying to get his hair to curl in the middle of his forehead like Nathan Collier's always does on TV). Mom and Dad were, of course, up in the cockpit, piloting us the 285 miles from Pisco to Cuzco.

"The indigenous people's name for the city of Cuzco was Qusqu, derived from the phrase *qusqu wanka* or 'rock of the owl.'"

"And the owl was sitting on a rock," said Chet.

"Very good," said Storm.

"Man, you know a lot of strange stuff, girl."

"Thank you," said Storm. "It's my superpower. Cuzco was also the Incan capital from the thirteenth century until the sixteenth century, when it was conquered by the Spanish. It's where Inkarri's arms might be buried."

"Wha-hut?" said Tommy.

Storm swiveled the screen of the computer around.

"Since this flight will take a few hours, I thought I would use the time productively and do more research on the Inkarri legend."

"Way to go, Stephanie!" said Mom from the front.

"Whoa," said Chet. "Your real name is Stephanie?"

"Yes," said Storm, those dark clouds filling her eyes again. "Say it again, Chester, and who knows where I might bury *your* arms."

"Riiiight. Gotcha. My bad."

"Tell us what you learned!" said Beck, because she likes horror stories way better than I do.

"As we already know," said Storm, "when the Spanish conquistadors tortured and executed the last Incan king, he vowed that he would one day rise up from his grave to avenge his death. To make sure that couldn't happen, the Spaniards buried his body parts all over Peru. According to my new research, legends claim that his head is under the presidential palace in Lima—"

"Great," said Mom. "That's where the big

rain-forest meeting is going to take place."

"Stay out of the basement, dear," joked Dad.

"His legs, some say," Storm continued, "went to Ayacucho, the capital of the Huamanga Province. His arms were buried under the Square of Tears in Cuzco."

"Let's not go there," said Tommy.

"Buried underground," said Storm, using her spooky voice, "all of Inkarri's body parts will grow back together, like the roots of a mighty tree, and when they do, he will rise up, take back his kingdom, and restore the harmony between Mother Earth and her children! Moo-hah-ha!"

CHAPTER 28

We all gave Storm a round of applause when she finished her in-flight entertainment.

"So," asked Chet, "why can't you guys hang out in Cuzco, take in all the top tourist sites? Why the big rush? We could pick up some good footage for the show. The Kidds kicking back and being the Kidds—"

"We may not be the only ones following this particular treasure map," said Mom.

"Fortunately," said Dad, patting his leather shoulder bag, which was draped over the back of his pilot's seat, "the other treasure hunters don't know precisely what they're looking for. A map isn't much good if you don't have the key."

"Cool," said Chet. "And you guys have the key? Is that what's in your bag, sir?"

"That information is currently classified," said Mom.

Hearing Mom say that made me feel way better. Chet Collier could film our treasure-hunting adventures all he wanted. But he couldn't know all of our family secrets—especially not the ones Dad figured out by reading that priest's letter we found on Cocos Island.

We landed at the airport in Cuzco.

Dad said we had "just enough time" to check out a few sights (because Mom never misses a chance for a quick homeschool field trip). Our first stop was an ancient Incan temple known as Quri-kancha, "the house of the sun."

"This was the most important temple in the Incan Empire," said Storm, our self-appointed family tour guide. "The walls were covered in sheets of gold. The courtyard was lined with golden statues."

Storm's fact-filled speech suddenly screeched to a halt when three menacing and extremely ancient-looking locals stepped out of the shadows.

CHAPTER 29

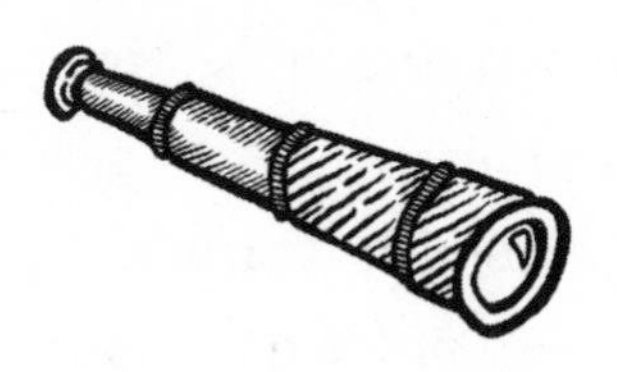

The three angry old men were dressed in traditional Quechuan costumes.

"The gold on the temple walls was our gold," said one.

"Which the Spaniards stole," said another.

"To melt down and send home to their king," said the third.

"Stay away from Paititi," said the first one.

"The Lost City of Gold belongs to us," said the second.

"It was a gift from Inkarri," said the third, who was the oldest and the scariest.

"We're not here to steal your gold," said Mom. "If we were to find—"

The oldest one raised his hand to cut her off.

"Stay away from Paititi, Kidd Family Treasure Hunters. The Home of the Jaguar Father holds many, many dangers. Those who search for it seldom come out of the jungle alive."

We all just stood there, stunned. I also gulped a little.

How could these three scary old men know who we were and what we were looking for? Had the bad guys from the submarine been here already? Did they figure out the owl-on-the-rock clue meant

Cuzco as quickly as Storm did? Had they told the angry old guys that we were on our way?

The three wrinkled men in their bright red costumes turned and disappeared into the shadows of the sun temple's ruins as eerily as they had arrived.

CHAPTER 30

"Soooo," said Chet after a prolonged silence. "Are you guys calling it quits and heading home? That's what my dad would do after running into those scary old dudes—"

"No way, Collier," said Tommy. "We're Kidds. We live for danger, action, and adventure. Right, Dad?"

"Indeed. However, Tommy, we need to tread most carefully. Our competitors in this quest have clearly spread false rumors about our intentions."

"It's too bad they turned the locals against us," said Mom with a sigh. "If we find the Lost City of Paititi, we plan on giving all the gold back to the people of Peru."

"You do?" said Chet, sounding surprised. "What is this? Catch-and-release treasure hunting?"

That made Dad laugh. "Something like that, Mr. Collier."

"My dad wouldn't do that either."

"Chya," said Tommy. "We know."

"Come along, everybody," said Dad, looking at his satellite phone. "It seems our local contact has procured ground transportation for us. We'll need it to head southeast into the rain forest."

"Is that where you guys are going next?" asked Chet, aiming his camera at Dad and then Storm.

Storm nodded. "According to the treasure map, we must hike through the cloud forests toward the morning sun."

"To find the Lost City of Paititi," said Dad, tapping his shoulder bag again, "we must first visit another ancient city."

"Machu Picchu?" I said—mostly to prove to Mom that I'd done my geography homework. "Is that what the priest's letter says?"

"No, Bick," said Dad. "Someplace altogether different and, at this point, unclear."

"Completely unclear," added Storm.

Bummer.

Machu Picchu—a fifteenth-century Incan citadel perched on a mountain peak eight thousand feet above sea level—is considered one of the Seven Wonders of the Modern World.

It's also Peru's number-one tourist attraction, so that meant there'd be a pretty easy way to get there. There'd probably be souvenir shops, too. And refreshing, ice-cold Coca-Cola.

Instead, we'd be heading in the opposite direction. Up into the mountains and the jungle.

The steep mountains. The muggy, sticky jungle.

Pack your antiperspirant, people. We're in for a sweat-fest.

"We'd better hurry," said Dad. "Our new friend says he'll wait for us at the historic Plaza de Armas with our transportation package."

"That's Cuzco's main square," said Storm, still in auto-tour-guide mode. "It's also known as Huacaypata, which translates to 'weeping square' or 'place of tears.'"

"Um, isn't that where you said they buried Inkarri's arms?" I asked.

"Exactly."

Storm. Always ready to tell you everything she knows even when you wish she wouldn't.

The seven of us hurried to the square. Nothing

spooky happened. No ghostly arms leaped up from under the cobblestones.

A man named Diego was waiting for us.

"Dr. Kidd, I presume?" he said to Dad.

"Yes, Diego. Thank you for making the arrangements for us."

"Jorge contacted me. Gave me your list of particulars. I trust you will find everything to your satisfaction."

I know I did.

Because there, in the square, were the two

most beautiful things Beck and I had seen since arriving in Peru.

I'm not talking about the twin cathedrals. Nope. What made our hearts skip a beat were parked behind a Toyota four-by-four: two quad ATVs!

One for Beck and one for me!

CHAPTER 31

We started loading gear into the back of the SUV.

"There won't be room for all seven of us inside the vehicle," said Dad.

"No problem," I said.

"Bick and I will gladly follow you guys on the quads," added Beck.

Dad grinned. "Such was my plan."

Beck and I put on helmets and eagerly climbed aboard our new rides. I could already hear their two-stroke engines whining like angry wasps, which was weird, because we hadn't even started them yet.

Suddenly a motorcycle roared up the street.

It whizzed by so fast and so close, my shirt ruffled in the breeze.

"He grabbed my bag!" shouted Dad.

"The priest's letter is inside it!" shouted Mom.

Beck and I didn't wait to hear what everybody else was going to shout.

We both locked our feet on the starters, gave a little jump, and pushed down hard. We each pulled in on the clutch, kicked the gear shifter into first, and blasted off. As we worked our way up the gear changes, I realized Dad had rented two very speedy all-terrain vehicles.

We chased the thief out of Cuzco, hoping that the rest of the family was chasing after us.

In no time, we were outside the city and in the open country. The mountains were spectacular.

We were also gaining on the guy.

The bag-snatcher veered off the road.

Beck and I did the same.

The bad guy skidded his dirt bike to a stop near a scaffold. He hopped off his ride and charged up what looked like a rolling section of bleacher steps.

"What is that thing?" cried Beck.

"Steps!" I shouted. Sunlight glinted off a taut wire. "To a zip line!"

As we raced closer, we passed a sign reading THE FLIGHT OF THE CONDOR. LONGEST ZIP LINE IN THE WORLD: 2,930 METERS.

"That's one-point-eight miles!" Beck shouted loudly. She's way faster at mathematical conversions than me.

The thief was strapping himself into a harness and shoving off from the platform.

"Looks like the line is broken up into sections," I said as Beck and I abandoned our ATVs and scampered up the scaffold. "There's a platform down there, maybe five hundred yards away, see it?"

"Not really, but I'll trust you. Let's go! Maybe we can tackle the guy before he clips onto the next section of wire!"

We tightened our helmets and slid into a pair of harnesses connected to one pulley.

"If we fly together, we'll fly faster," I said. "More weight equals more speed. That's just the law of gravity."

"Fine," said Beck as we bumped thighs. "Just try not to do anything too gassy."

"Deal!"

And then we leaped off the platform!

CHAPTER 32

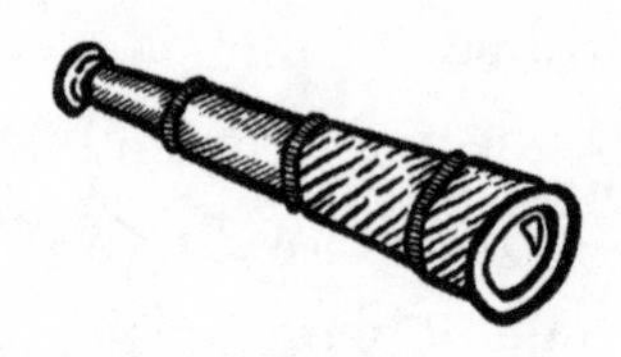

We sailed through the sky against the spectacular backdrop of the Maras mountains. It's a good thing me and Beck aren't afraid of heights.

The guy with Dad's bag reached the end of the first line and transferred to the second. We were maybe thirty seconds behind him when we quickly made the same switch, hooking our harnesses to the next set of wires.

Now we were flying above the Sacred Valley, known as the birthplace of the Incan Nation.

When we got to the transfer platform for the third cable, we were only ten seconds behind the thief. We made the change and zoomed along so fast, our cheeks started flapping in the breeze.

The bag man looked over his shoulder and saw that we were nearly close enough to reach out and grab Dad's satchel.

"¡Bueno!" he shouted. *"¡Usted puede tener la bolsa! ¡Es viejo y feo!"*

"He just called Dad's bag old and ugly," said Beck.

"Well, it sort of is..."

The flying purse-snatcher let go of Dad's shoulder bag.

Beck and I kicked out our legs and flapped our arms to slow ourselves down.

And watched the bag tumble down into the valley below.

Where Tommy and Storm were standing waiting to catch it like a high pop fly!

They had our twin ATVs. Guess they'd picked them up at that launchpad where we'd dropped them off.

We reached the transfer to the fourth cable—the longest and highest one in all of Peru—just as the local kleptomaniac took off. We were about to chase after him when Dad drove the SUV up and over the rugged ridge.

"Let him go!" shouted Mom as the vehicle swerved into a dusty fishtail. "He may be armed."

"You can stand down, kids," added Dad. "Storm and Tommy have retrieved my bag."

"And," said a very excited Chet Collier, "I recorded some excellent footage of you two soaring through the air like eagles."

"Condors," said Beck as we climbed down. "This is Peru. Condors fly over the Andes; eagles fly over the Rockies! Do a little homework, Chet."

I turned and watched the thief disappear. The fourth cable was over three-quarters of a mile long. The guy quickly turned into a hazy little blob.

"We should go after him," I said. "Find out why he stole your bag."

"Because he's a pickpocket and purse-snatcher," said Chet. "It's what they do, little dude."

Dad put his hand on my shoulder. "As much as I'd like to pursue the man who purloined my shoulder bag, Bick, I'm afraid he's flying in the wrong direction."

"We need to go south and then east to reach the rain forest," said Mom.

Tommy and Storm puttered up on the four-wheelers to join us.

"The, uh, you know, *thing* is safe, Dad," said Tommy, doing his best to speak in some kind of code. "He didn't steal anything, uh, *importante* out of your bag."

"Roger that," said Dad. "Well done, Bick and Beck. Thanks to you two, our mission remains on track. Our secret edge remains secure."

"Woo-hoo!" said Tommy. Then he started pumping his fist in the air. "U.S.A.! U.S.A.!"

Mom arched an eyebrow. "Thomas?"

"Sorry. My bad. Chase scenes always get me stoked."

PART II

TREASURE PIRATES

CHAPTER 33

We pushed on.

The trek through the mountains and into the rain forest took my breath away.

Literally.

The higher we climbed, the harder it was to breathe. The atmosphere kept getting thinner and thinner. I might've been getting thinner, too. If water makes up 60 percent of your body weight, I think I'd sweated out 30 percent of mine.

And then there were the llamas. We had to keep stopping so they could cross the washed-out roads we were traversing.

While we waited for the furry herd to clear the road, I remembered something Mom had told us: according to legends, Paititi was built by the Inca hero Inkarri, who had slipped away from the Spanish conquistadors with more than twenty thousand llamas loaded down with gold and silver!

Watching all those shaggy llama butts slowly making their way over the steep mountains, I realized we were probably headed in the right direction.

We might even be on the exact same route that Inkarri and his llamas took.

We were going to find the Lost City of Gold!

CHAPTER 34

We headed into the dense and drippy rain forest (what Storm's treasure map called the Cloud Forest).

Sadly, a lot of that forest had been chopped down.

"Half of Peru is covered with trees," said Mom as we studied the stumpy, lumber-littered landscape all around us. "Or at least it used to be. Nowadays, eleven thousand square miles of Peruvian forests are chopped down every year. And more than three-quarters of that deforestation is done illegally. This is what we need footage of, Chet. I want to take videos of this horrible destruction to Lima and plead with the president to step up his efforts to put a halt to it!"

"And," said Dad, "when we find the Lost City of Gold, the people of Peru can use that treasure to buy up more of the land to turn it into conservation areas."

"There's the sleeping lady," said Storm, gesturing to a mountain range above the tree line that, believe it or not, looked exactly like a woman taking a snooze.

Dad pulled the priest's letter out of his bag and consulted it. "We head in the direction the sleeping woman's toes point."

"Wha-hut?" said Beck.

"Check out that rocky outcropping at the end of the range," said Tommy. "That looks like a foot with stubby toes."

"They're aiming southeast," added Storm.

"So we drive southeast," said Dad.

"Oh, I get it now," said Chet. "You need the map and the letter. Otherwise you don't really know where you're supposed to go. Cool."

"Chet?" said Dad.

"Yes, sir?"

Dad gave Collier a super-stern look. "Kindly forget you ever figured that out."

"Yes, sir, Dr. Kidd, sir. Will do."

"But keep shooting video of these felled trees," urged Mom. "At the presidential summit, I'll be going up against Juan Carlos Rojas. I'll need all the evidence we can muster."

"Right," said Chet. "Who's this Rojas dude?"

"A bad guy," said Dad.

"The worst," said Mom. "A filthy-rich lumber baron who wants to buy up all of Peru's forestland for his own personal profit. Señor Rojas is a reckless, arrogant billionaire who once ordered his loggers to carve his initials into the forest so he could read them whenever he flew overhead in his private jet. I suspect he is the illegal hand behind this horrible devastation."

"You're probably right," I said. "I think we're standing in the curved bottom of a *J* right now. Could be a *C*—"

We heard branches snap.

Somewhere in the thick foliage surrounding the clearing, another two-cylinder engine sputtered and chugged to life.

This one wasn't on an ATV or a dirt bike.

This one had the unmistakable sound of a chain saw!

CHAPTER 35

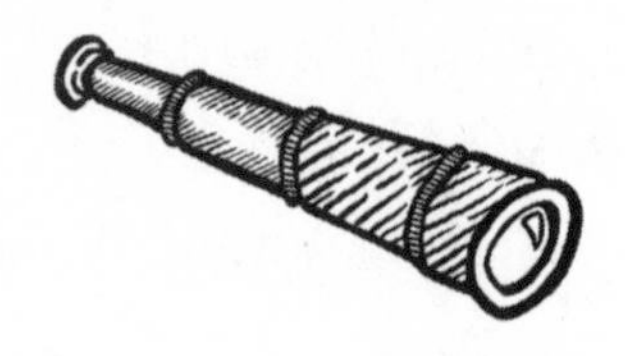

Suddenly, a group of scary-looking men lugging chain saws and rifles strode into the clearing.

"What are you Yanquis doing here in Señor Rojas's forest?" asked the leader after he shut down his saw. He wore a red T-shirt as a mask and spoke pretty good English. "For it can be a very dangerous place."

"This isn't Señor Rojas's forest," said Mom defiantly. "It belongs to the people of Peru."

The man laughed. "Not for long. Señor Rojas is going to buy it from El Presidente!"

"Not if we offer a better price!"

"And what would you do with these trees, Yanqui lady?"

"Protect them!"

"Ha," the man sneered. "Señor Rojas brings jobs to the people. What do the trees bring besides bugs and snakes? You will never outbid Señor Rojas. You will lose!"

You know how my big sister's eyes get all dark and stormy whenever she's mad?

I think Storm inherited that trait from Mom.

Because after the logger thug said that, thunderstorm warnings were definitely issued for Mom's eyeballs.

"You can't scare me or my family, sir," said Mom.

"Is that so?" said the logger. "Because that was my plan. Boo!"

The crew behind him laughed.

"But, my Yanqui friend," he went on, "if I cannot scare you, perhaps the rain forest you love so much will. Beware. Danger lurks around every tree."

He motioned to his men. They all yanked up on their starter cords. Five chain saws roared to life. Dad motioned for all of us to stand behind him and Tommy as they formed a protective barricade between us and the malicious loggers.

"For instance," the masked man hollered over the rattling din, "do not pick fruit from a palm tree. Snakes will hide in the warmth of the dry leaves at the base of the tree. The snakes will bite your ankle. They will sink their teeth into your flesh just like this."

He dipped the nose of his chain saw into the front tire of the SUV while three of his friends did the same to the other wheels. They sliced the vehicle's tires into rubber shreds.

"If you pick fruit from a lemon or orange tree," shouted the masked man, "be especially careful. The sweeter the fruit, the more likely the tree will be home to a wasps' nest. You do not want to anger the wasps, my friends. Their stingers are very, very sharp. Just like the blades of our saws!"

This time, they attacked our twin quads, ripping all the tires to bits.

"Most of all, when in this misty green world, do not offend those who have been here much, much longer than you. The jaguars. The snakes. And us!"

The men laughed and, chain saws still rumbling and rattling, marched off into the forest, leaving us stranded in the middle of all those fallen trees, jaguars, snakes, and wasps.

CHAPTER 36

"So *now* do you guys call it quits?" asked Chet, aiming his camera at Dad.

"Of course not, Mr. Collier," said Dad calmly. "We will forge ahead on foot until alternative forms of transportation can be procured."

"Um, Dad?" said Tommy. "Not for nothing, but I don't think there are any SUV dealerships in the middle of the Peruvian rain forest."

"Maybe we could patch the tires," I suggested.

"They chewed them to pieces with their saws, Bick," said Beck.

"True. So it would be a ginormous patch job. Maybe we could find a rubber tree—"

"You can't just take the bark of a rubber tree and retread a tire, Bickford!"

"Well, Rebecca, I don't hear you coming up with a better idea!"

We were about to break into another Twin Tirade when the leaves started rustling ominously again.

A group of what I figured had to be locals stepped into the clearing. They looked like a family, all of them dressed in a mix of modern and traditional clothing of the indigenous people. Oh, *indigenous* is one of those words Mom taught us when we were, like, six. It means "the original or native people." The ones who have been living somewhere even longer than a masked maniac with a chain saw.

None of our new visitors were carrying logging equipment or rifles, although the man who looked like the head of the group *was* wearing a traditional feathered headdress.

WELCOME TO OUR HOME. SORRY IT IS SO MESSY. TOO MANY LOGGERS HAVE BEEN VISITING LATELY.
MY VOW TO NOT FALL IN LOVE IS ABOUT TO GET CHOPPED DOWN, TOO!

"Are you here with Juan Carlos Rojas's men to destroy our ancestral home?" asked the man wearing the feathered crown.

"On the contrary," said Mom. "We are here to do everything we can to put a stop to this deforestation and to Señor Rojas's plans."

The man smiled. "Then you are most welcome. Please. Come journey with us to our village for food and rest."

"Chya," said Tommy, smiling at the very pretty teenage girl traveling with the group. "I could totally use some rest and relaxation. So, what do they call you, besides beautiful?"

Chet stepped up beside Tommy. "I think they also call her gorgeous."

Tommy looked at Chet. "Whoa. Ease up, dude."

"Sorry, Tommy. No can do. Besides, you're out of your league, kid."

"Watch it, Collier!"

The girl laughed. "My name is Q'orianka," she said with a soft smile. "It means 'golden eagle' in Quechua."

"Well, hello, Golden Eagle," said Chet, twisting

his ruby class ring, I guess because he thought it made him look suave and sophisticated. “You’re definitely one pretty birdie.”

Q’orianka rolled her eyes. She was already over Chet. Tommy saw his opening!

“Um, I’m Tommy. It’s short for Thomas. Like the train.”

“Actually,” said Storm, “Thomas is derived from a Greek word for ‘twin,’ which he isn’t.”

“But we are,” I said, gesturing to Beck. “I’m Bick. This is my twin sister, Beck.”

“That’s our mom and dad,” said Beck. “We’re the Kidds.”

“Chet isn’t one of us,” I explained.

“He’s a Collier,” said Tommy. This time he almost gagged on the *K* sound.

“You are all welcome in our village,” said the man in the ceremonial headdress. “I am the village president, Chaupi. Come. We will send others to tend to your vehicles.”

“Will they be safe here?” asked Dad.

Chaupi shook his head. “This is the jungle, my new friend. Nothing and no one is ever safe.”

CHAPTER 37

We followed Chaupi deeper and deeper into the rain forest. The trail took us over rickety boardwalks and a winding path through huge mounds of dirt and rocks.

"Left over from illegal gold mines," explained Chaupi as he led us through the leafy forest.

"Speaking of gold," I whispered to Storm, "are we still going the right way to find you-know-where?"

"Yes," she whispered back. "In fact, there was a marking on the map suggesting that we would pass through a small village on our journey."

"Cool!"

"But the symbol after that is one I don't understand at all."

"Don't worry," I told her. "It'll come to you. It always does."

My compliment seemed to surprise Storm. "Thank you, Bick. I hope it will."

Finally, a very sweaty hour later, we arrived at a small cluster of homes made of bare boards. The thatched-roof shacks were bunched together at the edge of a muddy river. I was super-glad there was a covered shelter we could all squeeze into because as soon as we reached the village, it started raining.

"Our ancestors have lived in this clearing for many centuries," said Chaupi over the pattering of the torrential downpour.

"However," said the young girl Q'orianka, "we may not be able to live here much longer."

Chaupi rested his hand on the head of the youngest member of his family—a son who looked to be maybe six years old.

"What my oldest and wisest daughter says is true," he said. "With so many trees being cut down, the sun is much stronger than it was when I was a boy growing up in this valley. Now, the sun feels so close, it burns our skin. It is as if the sun god is angry at those who have ruined our land and taken away his gift of the trees. Without a canopy of leaves over our heads, the sun beats down mercilessly, drying out the fruit and the fishes and the birds, making everything so much smaller. Without the trees' roots gripping the ground, the very earth is in danger of washing away."

"It makes me wish the legends of Inkarri were true!" added Q'orianka. "That he would rise up from the dead and restore the earth to peace and harmony for the people of Peru!"

"Well," said Mom, "I may not be able to rise up from the earth like Inkarri could, but I can most definitely stand up to the powerful logging lobby in Lima."

As the rain kept beating down in unrelenting sheets, she told our hosts about the big rain-forest conference that was coming up at the presidential palace.

"Here in this village," she said, "you are dealing with the consequences of deforestation on a daily basis."

"This is why I must come with you to Lima," said Chaupi. "And voice our concerns."

"I would be honored to have you travel with me, Chaupi," said Mom. "You will speak more eloquently than I ever could!"

"I just hope it is not too little too late," said Chaupi.

That's when his son shrieked and pointed uphill to a roiling wall of swirling mud.

"Flash flood!" screamed Chaupi. "Head to higher ground or you will all be washed away!"

Chaupi and his children led us up a hill.

Until a wall of water rolled over them and swept away his youngest son!

CHAPTER 38

"Yacu!" shouted Chaupi as the mud-choked floodwaters carried his little boy downhill toward the river.

"Tayta!" screamed the boy.

The churning current dragged him along like driftwood.

"Come on, Beck!" I hollered. "Time to swim like we're in shark-infested waters again!"

"Right behind ya!"

"Wait, you two!" shouted Dad.

We disobeyed Dad's order and dove into the

muddy gully washer as it streaked down the slick slope toward the swollen river. I could see Yacu's head bobbing in the choppy waves.

"Hang on, Yacu!" I cried. "We're coming!"

Since Beck and I were the closest in age and weight to the six-year-old boy, the rushing flood seemed to carry us along at almost the same pace as it was carrying him. Fortunately, all those years living on the *Lost* had made us both excellent swimmers—no matter the conditions.

While I kicked my legs and worked my arms, I couldn't help thinking that this was what happened when you chopped down way too many trees in the rain forest: there weren't enough roots in the ground to stop the earth from sloughing off and washing away in a downpour.

Behind me, I heard a mighty crunch and a jumble of twisting snaps.

I glanced over my shoulder.

The flood had just bowled down the shelter we'd all been standing under and sent it sailing toward us.

"We can use this!" I said.

"How?" cried Beck.

"We can ride the roof downstream to rescue Yacu!"

"Good idea."

Beck and I swam over to the floating hut and hauled ourselves up onto its slanted top.

"Hang on, Yacu!" I cried. "We're coming!"

"And," added Beck, "we're bringing a boat. A houseboat!"

Beck lay facedown on the roof. She jabbed

her feet through the thatching and braced them against a beam. I walked along the peak until I reached the edge of the roof, right in front of Beck.

"Grab my ankles!" I shouted.

"Got 'em!"

The hut swung sideways. We were parallel with the boy being washed downstream in the raging rapids.

With Beck holding my legs, I crouched down.

Yacu was coughing and spitting out everything the angry river was forcing him to swallow.

I lunged forward. Beck tightened her grip.

I went underwater for a swirling second but sprang right back up to the surface.

I grabbed Yacu's hand. He grabbed mine.

I pulled Yacu up to the roof.

He was shivering, but he was safe.

He hugged me. I hugged him back.

“I’ve got you,” I told him. “And I’m not letting go!”

The rain stopped as quickly as it had begun.

Our floating shed snagged itself on a dam of rocks and mud and lumber that the flood had left in its wake.

The sun peeked through the clouds. When it did, I realized why the ancient Incas might’ve worshipped it—because the sun usually brings good things and puts an end to the bad ones.

Like the rains that tried to wash away our new friend’s youngest son.

CHAPTER 39

Dad gave Beck and me a little grief about doing something so dangerous. "We're better when we all work together," he told us. "Think about that before you two jump into danger headfirst again."

"Yes, sir," we both said, even though, between you and me, I think Beck and I did an amazingly spectacular job on our own.

That night, after the sun spent the day drying out the village, we had a huge celebration. All the locals put on their most festive feathered costumes. They cooked us a feast, banged drums, tooted wooden flutes, and danced. Beck and I were given feathered necklaces and crowns.

WOW! I'M A HERO.
BOOM! BOOM! BOOM!
GOOD. BECAUSE YOU'RE DEFINITELY NOT A DANCER.
BANG BANG BOOM!
RATTLE RATTLE RATTLE

"These two, the twins, saved my son," Chaupi announced. "From this day forward, they are both honorary members of the Harakmbut people! Anything you need, ask, and it will be given to you!"

"Woo-hoo!" Beck and I shouted.

Tommy was dancing with Q'orianka. We found out that, while we had been saving Yacu, Tommy was saving Q'orianka. He apparently squirmed out of his pants while treading water, tied off the ends of the pant legs, zipped up the zipper, waved the pants over his head to fill them with air, knotted off the waist to trap as much air as he could, and then handed the bubble-butted khaki balloon to Q'orianka for her to use as a flotation device.

"You know," he told Q'orianka as they slow-danced together to the haunting flute music, "I'd fall in love with you right now but I promised my family I wouldn't have any more girlfriends for at least a month."

"I am sorry to hear that, Thomas," said Q'orianka. "Because you are my hero. I thank you and your pants for saving my life."

"Ah, what the heck," said Tommy. "One day with you is worth a month with anyone else. Everybody, I'm officially in love again!"

"Whoa, hang on, dude," said Chet Collier, trying to cut in on Tommy and Q'orianka's dance. "What about me, sweet eagle girl?"

"You?" she said. "When the floodwaters rose, you climbed a banyan tree."

"Chya," said Tommy. "Totally."

"I only did it to make sure the branches were safe enough for you to climb up and join me, my dear."

Chet wiggled his eyebrows. Q'orianka laughed. Then she and Tommy danced away together.

Meanwhile, Storm sat on a fallen log, drawing something in the dirt with a stick. Everybody else was celebrating, but she was pouting. Beck and I went over to check out the situation.

"What's wrong?" I asked.

"I'm still stumped," said Storm. "This 'village of the feathered ones' is definitely on the map. But I don't understand where we're supposed to go next. I can't find the lost city we need to go to before we can reach the City of Gold."

"What's the hieroglyph?" asked Beck.

Storm tapped the symbol she had etched in the dirt.

It looked like a ball sitting on a diving board or the bottom step of a staircase.

Chaupi strolled over to see what we were all staring at.

"Ah," he said. "The city of the *uqha pacha*."

"Huh?" I said.

"That is the top-right section of a *chakana,* or Incan cross," he explained. "It has many meanings for us. In this section of the cross, we see the three levels of life: heaven on the top step, the earth in the middle, and the underworld, or *uqha pacha,* below."

"Huh," said Storm. "I did not know that."

(Guess there's a first time for everything.)

"This is the next symbol on our treasure map," I explained.

"Then, my friends, you do not have far to journey." Chaupi pointed to the east. "Your map is sending you to a nearby necropolis."

"What's that?" asked Beck.

The elder's face grew very serious. "The Lost City of the Dead. The home of the Sacred Stone."

CHAPTER 40

The next morning, as we were packing our gear, some villagers emerged from the jungle carrying a pair of wounded beasts, each tied to a pole.

Our ATVs!

"You saved my son," explained Chaupi, "so we will repair your vehicles. We will send for new tires while you journey to the Lost City of the Dead."

"Thanks, bro! Oh, what about the SUV?" asked Tommy.

"It was too wide for us to carry along the narrow paths," said Chaupi. "Most unfortunate."

Beck and I were still feeling like total heroes for saving Yacu's life. And now we were getting our rides back! Plus, they'd given us those feathered necklaces, each one decorated with a golden medallion.

"The left leg, and the right leg," Chaupi had told us when he draped the gold medals around our necks like we were Olympic champions. To be honest, the images carved in gold didn't really resemble limbs. To me, they looked more like tiny tables or weird chess pieces with toes.

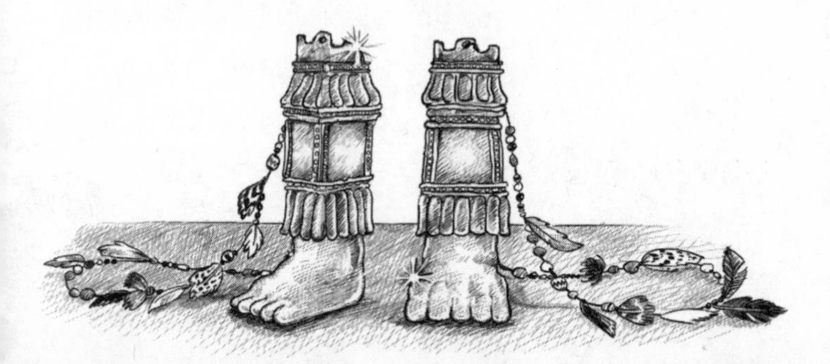

I wasn't exactly sure why the village president wanted to give Beck and me an antique set of golden legs. Maybe because we'd kicked the flood's butt. Or because we danced with danger. Something epic and leggish like that.

"The amulets you wear have been in our village for many centuries," Chaupi told us.

"Inkarri!" mumbled one of the elders. "Inkarri!"

"What's he saying?" asked Dad.

Chaupi smiled kindly at the old man. "Legend has it that Inkarri—or one of his most loyal followers—left the golden medallions here in our village for safekeeping. That he would come back and reclaim them after he rose from the dead."

"Then we should give these back to you," I said.

"Definitely," added Beck. "We don't want to upset a dead guy. Especially if he's coming back."

We both went to lift our nifty new lanyards over our heads.

Chaupi held up his hand. "No. They are my gift. May they protect you as you protected my son."

"We'll bring them back," said Dad. "After we complete our quest."

"We'll trade 'em in for the ATVs!" I added.

Chaupi grinned. "Very well."

His grin faded fast.

"But wear them this day as you venture deeper into the jungle. For you will need all possible protection as you approach the necropolis—the Lost City of the Dead."

The way he said that?

Somebody should've added a spooky *"Dun-dun-dun!"*

CHAPTER 41

We were trudging through the sweltering jungle when I heard a strange blurp of a chirp.

I thought maybe it was a Peruvian monkey's mating call.

Then I realized the thing making the noise was zipped inside Mom's backpack.

"I hope that's not an angry monkey," I said.

"Sounds more like a sick parakeet," said Beck.

"Well," said Storm, shifting into her rain-forest tour-guide mode, "this particular jungle region is home to a wide and wonderful diversity of birds. It could be a yellow-billed jacamar, a yellow-rumped cacique, a golden-headed manakin..."

She probably could've gone on for hours. (She usually does.) But Mom finally pulled the annoying blurper out of her pack and raised her hand for silence. The thing that was making the noise was a jumbo-size satellite phone. It looked like a black brick with a stubby antenna—one of the older models. I figured she'd bought it on sale at a CIA Spy Store clearance sale.

"This is Sue Kidd," she said into the phone.

She listened intently. The rest of us waited to find out who was calling Mom in the middle of the Peruvian rain forest.

"But the meeting was supposed to be next week. Oh. I see. Señor Rojas won't be available next week? He demands that the meeting take place tomorrow? Ha! That's ridiculous."

There was a pause as Mom's jaw dropped.

"It's set for noon? But we don't have the additional resources we discussed. We haven't found the gold..."

Mom sighed. Pinched that spot on her nose

between her eyeballs that she always pinches when she has to make a tough decision.

"Have them send in the bird," she told whoever was on the other end of the line. "I'll fly to Lima immediately. A local leader named Chaupi will be traveling with me. He knows more about the impact of deforestation than anybody."

Yeah, I thought. *He almost lost his son to it.*

"Maybe the two of us can buy some extra time while my family continues on to Paititi," Mom said. "We have a high degree of confidence that we will soon find the gold we need to outbid Rojas and preserve the land for the Peruvian people."

Whoa. I liked hearing that.

But not all the other stuff. Because it sounded like Mom would be leaving us (again) and heading to the capital of Peru to meet with big-time government officials plus our main rain-forest rival, Juan Carlos Rojas.

"You think we'll ever do a complete treasure hunt as a whole family again?" Beck whispered to me as Mom ended her satellite-phone call.

"We all have different jobs to do on this team, Rebecca," said Dad, because Beck isn't the quietest whisperer in the world. "If your mother needs to go with Chaupi to Lima, then that's where she'll go."

Then he reminded us of our new primary mission: to save the most precious treasure on the planet—the planet itself.

"Chet?" Mom said to Collier.

"Yes, Mrs. Kidd?"

"Keep recording any rain-forest devastation you guys see. Beam it up to the Cloud. I'll download it onto my laptop in Lima and share it with the president and interior minister."

"You got it, Mrs. Kidd," said Chet.

That meant Chet wasn't choppering out with Mom. Too bad. I'd kind of hoped someone would beam him up to a cloud. I still didn't trust the guy. He was a Collier. He wasn't family.

Thirty minutes later, the leaves and trees around us started swaying as a helicopter hovered overhead. There was no place for it to land, so the pilot lowered a rope ladder.

"We'll double back to the village," Mom shouted over the rotor wash. "Pick up Chaupi."

"Good luck," said Dad, giving her a kiss.

Mom grabbed hold of the rope ladder and climbed up into the green canopy of fluttering foliage.

It reminded me of the way Dad had left us one stormy night aboard the *Lost,* even though none of us had seen him go.

CHAPTER 42

"So what do you know about this Sacred Stone?" asked Chet Collier as we hiked up a steep and steamy hill.

He had his camera trained on Storm.

"We know it is sacred," said Storm. "And that it's a stone."

(Have I mentioned that Storm isn't exactly crazy about being on camera?)

"But what does it have to do with finding Paititi, the Lost City of Gold?"

"We won't know the significance of the stone, Chet, until we secure it," said Dad, coming to Storm's rescue. "However, according to a letter written by a Spanish missionary named Father Toledo and addressed to 'His Holiness, the Pope,' once we find the Sacred Stone, *todo será revelado.*"

"That's Spanish," said Tommy. "Because the priest was, like, from Spain and they used to speak Spanish in Spain. Still do."

"Indeed," said Dad, arching an eyebrow, marveling at Tommy's illogical logic.

"Well, what exactly do those Spanish words mean?" asked Chet.

"'All shall be revealed,'" replied Dad. "Let us hope such will be the case."

"Why?" I asked.

"Because that is the final instruction in Father Toledo's letter to the pope."

"Wait a second," said Tommy. "There aren't any more bonus clues?"

Dad shook his head. "I'm afraid not."

"Bummer."

"Then this stone must be super-important," said Beck.

"Exactly," Dad said. "I suspect it might be a lodestone."

"You mean like real heavy rock?" I asked. "A real load?"

"No, Bick," said Tommy. "A lodestone is a naturally occurring magnetized rock that ancient mariners used to use to make primitive compasses so they could navigate in waters far away from any land."

Yep, there's one subject where Tommy is actually more of an expert than Storm: boat driving.

"The Vikings used to glue a lodestone on top of a chunk of wood and float it in a bucket of water," he said. "Because it was magnetized, the lodestone would always point toward magnetic north."

"Exactly, Thomas," said Dad. "If we find the Sacred Stone, I suspect it will, somehow, point us to Paititi."

We kept hiking. And hacking machetes against ropy vines. And chopping floppy leaves. And slicing through wet green stuff.

For hours and hours. My legs and my arms were killing me.

Storm noticed a few more landmarks from her memorized map. She assured us we were heading in the right direction. Unfortunately, that direction was deeper and deeper into the rain forest. I had so many mosquito bites, my knees looked like they had acne.

Just when I didn't think I could take another inch of jungle, it ended.

We stepped into a clearing and faced a sheer cliff of weathered volcanic rock. Dozens of openings that looked like windows were chiseled into the stone. It was kind of like staring at a ginormous skull with too many eye sockets. Or a honeycomb made out of concrete. Either way, it was spooky.

"Each one of those niches was a tomb," explained Storm. "Or an entrance into a deeper tomb. The City of the Dead was built by an ancient Andean civilization that lived here long before the Incas."

"They probably died here, too," quipped Beck. "I'm guessing that's why they needed so many tombs."

"And," said Dad, "much like the ancient Egyptians, these ancient Andeans thought death was merely a continuation of life. Therefore, they placed pottery, utensils, food, and, yes, even jewelry inside the funeral niches with the remains of their dearly departed loved ones."

"So that's where you'll find the Sacred Stone?" said Chet. "In one of those holes?"

Dad just nodded.

Meanwhile, my stomach lurched up into my mouth.

I had a queasy feeling that, to find the key to the Lost City of Paititi, we were going to have to crawl through a bunch of creepy caves crammed full of even creepier skeletons.

CHAPTER 43

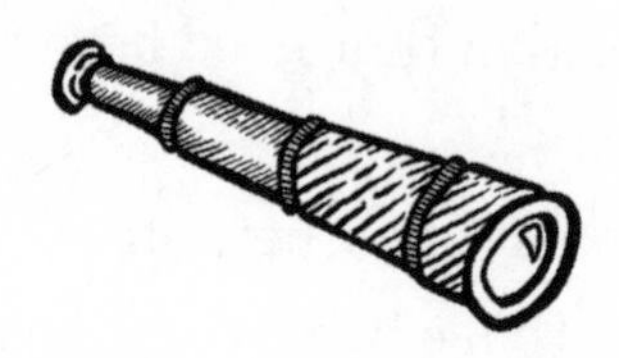

"Do we have any idea which one of those holes we're supposed to crawl into?" asked Beck.

"No," said Dad. "So we need to split up into teams. Beck and Bick? You're together. Start on the top level and work your way from left to right."

"Yes, sir," I said. I even saluted.

"Tommy and Storm? I want you guys to take the lowest tier. Move right to left."

"Gotcha," said Tommy.

Storm raised a hand.

"Yes, Storm?" said Dad.

"Can Tommy do most of the crawling? I'm wearing shorts. I really don't want to scrape my shins on broken bones and pottery shards."

"Of course. But Storm? Keep your eyes open for the Sacred Stone."

"Got it."

Dad turned to Collier. "Chet? You'll be with me. We'll work the middle row of caves."

"Cool."

"If you find the stone, give the family whistle," said Dad to everyone.

We all nodded. Except, of course, Chet. He wasn't in our family. He didn't know the secret whistle or our secret handshake.

"Um, what's the whistle sound like?" asked Chet.

"You need not worry," Dad told him. "If you and I find something, I'll give the whistle. All right. It could be a tight squeeze in those niches. We'd better stow our gear down here."

We all slipped off our backpacks and set them on the dusty ground.

"Whoa," said Tommy, who, by the way, is an excellent tracker. "Are those footprints?"

Dad knelt down and examined the markings Tommy was pointing to.

"Worse," said Dad. "Those are boot prints. Judging by the tread marks, I'd say they are high-end hiking boots, the kind one might purchase at an expedition outfitter."

"So they likely weren't worn by the locals," I said.

"You are correct," said Storm. "Most indigenous people in the Andes wear *hojotas,* which are sandals made from recycled tires."

"Precisely," said Dad.

"Could it be those other guys?" said Beck, looking around nervously. "The submarine pirates who stole the treasure map out of the Room on the *Lost*?"

"Impossible," said Storm. "Even though they had the map, they didn't have Father Toledo's letter. They wouldn't've known what to do with the landmarks, such as the sleeping-lady mountain."

"With the pointing toes!" added Tommy.

"What if Father Toledo sent two letters to the pope?" I wondered out loud. "What if he made a copy and stored it someplace else? Someplace where the bad guys found it."

"I suppose that's a possibility, Bick," said Dad. "So let's work fast and keep our eyes and ears open. The Sacred Stone is the key to the city of Paititi. We can't let it fall into the wrong hands!"

We all hustled off to our assigned slots.

Beck and I clambered up the sides of the necropolis and crawled into our first tomb on the top row.

It wasn't too scary. Unless, of course, you don't particularly enjoy wriggling along on your belly on top of a bed of scattered skeletons.

CHAPTER 44

Beck and I were in our third tomb when we discovered (accidentally) the first booby trap.

I threw a chunk of broken pottery to scare off a pack of squeaking rats ten feet in front of us. It must've hit a trip wire as it tumbled through the air because, all of a sudden, dozens of pointy-tipped darts shot across the cave in both directions.

"Um, I think those were meant for us," mumbled Beck. "Let's get out of here."

"No," I said, sort of surprising myself by saying it. "We have to explore this cave."

“What? Are you crazy? Do you want to trigger some other kind of crazy trap? Maybe even a giant rolling rock like in that movie you watch all the time?”

It’s true. I’m a huge *Raiders of the Lost Ark* fan.

“Think about it, Beck,” I told her. “There weren’t any booby traps in the first two tombs we explored.”

“True. Just spooky skeletons and squiggly snakes.”

“And cobwebs,” I reminded her. “And humongous furry spiders.”

“Yeah. Those were gross.”

“But,” I said, “this is the first tomb with man-made hazards.”

“Well, maybe the dead guy’s family was super-protective. Didn’t want grave robbers messing with their dearly departed loved one’s pottery and stuff.”

“Or maybe this is a passageway that will lead us to something super-special. Something that required extra security.”

Beck's eyes lit up. "The Sacred Stone."

"Exactly."

"We should whistle for the others," said Beck.

"Not yet," I said. "What if we're wrong?"

"You usually are."

"No, I'm not."

"Yes. You are."

We were dangerously close to launching into a fresh Twin Tirade, which would have been very hard to accomplish in such a cramped space. Tirades usually involved a lot of flailing arms, and we didn't have room for that. Plus, we didn't have time for a tirade. If the Sacred Stone wasn't in this booby-trapped tomb, we had at least a dozen more to explore. So did Storm and Tommy, and Dad and Chet.

"We have to do this on our own," I said.

"Fine," said Beck with an exasperated sigh. "Just be careful."

We crawled forward, past the piles of spiky darts littering both sides of the tomb tunnel. Bones and shards of clay crunched under our hands and knees. I brought my right hand down on a dusty stone. Beside me, Beck rested her hand on a skull.

The skull sank into the floor.

“Uh-oh,” she mumbled.

We heard heavy stones scraping and clunking together like prehistoric cogwheels and gears.

We also heard a horrible hissing sound coming from behind us.

“Um, Bick?”

“Yeah?”

“Is there, like, a giant snake back there?”

“I don’t know. I’m too afraid to look.”

“Me, too,” said Beck.

“We should probably do it together.”

“Yeah. On three. One…two…three.”

We both turned around and looked back to where we’d been.

The holes in the stone walls where all those darts had come flying out of were now leaking a thick, pea-green gas cloud.

The skull had been a trigger for booby trap number two!

“That’s some kind of poisonous gas!” Beck gasped.

I fanned the air under my nose. “Either that or the walls just farted.”

One thing was clear: We couldn’t go out the way we’d come in without running through (and breathing in) the gas cloud. We had to crawl deeper into the cave.

"It's not all bad," I said.

"What?" shouted Beck.

"Hey, if the gas kills us, at least we're already in a tomb!"

CHAPTER 45

Call us crazy, but Beck and I decided to run.

Luckily, the cave ceiling became higher up ahead. We didn't trigger any more booby traps—probably because whoever installed the dart launchers and the gas pumpers figured those two items would be more than enough to take care of any and all grave robbers.

And because they also probably knew we'd run into a wall.

Which is what we did. There was no rear exit. Just a tall stone wall.

"What's that?" said Beck, shining her flashlight on a carving at the base of the wall.

"Some kind of Incan art," I said. "Too bad we don't have time for an art-appreciation class right now, Rebecca. We need to find a way out before that poison-gas cloud finds its way into this room."

"Fascinating," mumbled Beck, sounding like Mom when she's in an art museum admiring a masterpiece.

"Hello? Earth to Beck? We're about ten seconds

away from dying a horrible, miserable death. I'm talking choking and gagging and bloodshot eyeballs."

"It's Incan art," she replied, because, as the family artiste, she pays more attention during Mom's art history lectures than I do. "Very curious."

"What?"

"Storm and Dad said these tombs were built by a pre-Incan civilization."

"So?"

"Pre-Incan means it came before the Incas. So why is there Incan art decorating this wall?"

Okay. She had a point. She might not have had very long to live, but she had a point.

"It looks like a solar disk," she went on while I waved at the foul air tickling my nostrils. The stinky gas was seeping into the back chamber where we were trapped. "The sun, of course, is a very important symbol in Incan mythology."

"Of course," I said, coughing a little. My eyes started stinging.

"Beneath the solar disk, we see two kneeling figures on either side of a diamond-shaped object. It's almost as if they are worshipping the diamond."

"Well, maybe it's some kind of sacred stone," I said without thinking.

"Exactly," said Beck, smiling, which I thought was a very odd thing to be doing ten seconds before you died dramatically and horribly in a poisonous-gas attack.

Then she did something even weirder: she placed her thumb against the carved image of the sun.

I heard another clunk and clink of stone sliding against stone.

Finally, I figured out what Beck already had. "The Sacred Stone!"

"Exactly!"

We heard more grinding. And rumbling. Centuries-old dust puffed out of cracks in the trembling walls. We both looked up at the ceiling, terrified it would collapse on us.

The floor flew open beneath our feet.

We both screamed as we disappeared through the trapdoor and into the darkness below. We fell, weightless, for a few seconds, then landed hard on our butts and flew down a slanted stone chute. It was like riding along on a slippery waterslide but without the water, just a thick layer of dust.

"At least the air smells better in here," shouted Beck as we swerved through a curve and skimmed through what might've been the dry and dusty sewer pipes of the City of the Dead.

CHAPTER 46

Finally, after a few more twists and turns and scraped elbows (not to mention sore butts), we flew out of the stone chute and landed on a heap of something soft.

"Okay," said Beck. "That was convenient."

"Or planned," I said, fingering the fuzzy pile of padding. "I think this might be antique llama wool."

Beck snapped her fingers. "Inkarri used twenty thousand llamas to transport all that gold and silver to Paititi. His followers probably gave the herd a few haircuts and made this landing cushion when they decided to hide their Sacred Stone deep within this old necropolis."

"We took the path they planned to take when Inkarri came back to reclaim his treasure," I added. "They would've known about the booby traps and how *not* to trigger them."

I shone my flashlight right. Beck shone hers left. It's a twin thing.

My beam fell on a wall painting.

"It's a map!" I said. "No, it's *the* map. The same one Storm drew for us on her computer. The one the bad guys stole out of the Room."

"And that," said Beck, "must be the Sacred Stone."

"Whaaa—"

I spun around to see what she was talking about.

There it was. A glittering, faceted yellow stone the size of a baseball sitting on a pedestal that had more of those kneeling Incan figures carved into its sides.

"No wonder they put it on a pedestal!" said Beck, her voice filled with awe.

Beck grabbed the stone before I could tell her not to (because, like I said, I've seen way more Indiana Jones movies than she has).

And, of course, the column started to rise. Once again, we heard the grind and scrape of stone against stone.

"Is the floor going to open up again?" sputtered Beck, backing up against the far wall.

"I hope not," I told her. "But the weight of the Sacred Stone was keeping the column locked in place. You were supposed to put a bag of sand that weighed as much as it did on top of the pedestal before you grabbed the shiny stone!"

"Sorry."

The column kept corkscrewing up from the floor. And that wall Beck had backed up against? It started slowly sliding open, disappearing into the rock like a pocket door.

"Bick? Beck?"

Tommy and Storm were standing on the other side of the sliding wall in what had to be a tomb on the level they'd been exploring. I could see a brilliant rectangle of blinding sunlight behind them.

"How'd you guys get down here?" asked Tommy.

"Very quickly," said Beck.

"But this is our level," said Storm. "Besides, you were supposed to whistle if you found something."

Beck whistled. It was a very dry, very weak whistle.

"Is that the Sacred Stone?" asked Storm,

clumping into the chamber to join us. Tommy was right behind her.

"We think so," said Beck.

"And check it out," I said. "There's a map painted on the wall!"

Storm scanned the cave painting.

"It's a perfect match," she reported after comparing it to the visual files in her ginormous brain. "It's exactly the same as the map Dad had on board the *Lost*."

"Awesome," said Tommy.

"Wow," said Beck. "There's like a dozen of you guys."

Storm, Tommy, and I turned away from the wall map to check out Beck.

She had the Sacred Stone pressed against her eye and was staring through it as if it were a telescope.

Tommy shook his head.

"You really shouldn't be playing with that," he said, moving away from the wall to go retrieve the stone.

Beck gasped.

"You guys?" she said, still staring through the stone. "You're not going to believe what I just saw!"

"What?"

"The Lost City of Paititi!"

CHAPTER 47

"Remember that time on the *Lost* when I looked at one of Dad's maps while wearing my three-D glasses?" said Beck, still gaping at the painting on the sleek cavern wall.

"Of course we do," I said. "You found the map Dad had drawn with some kind of invisible ink that could only be seen if you were wearing those stupid goggles you wore all the time."

"Chya," said Tommy. "And the hidden map led us all the way to New York City and the Grecian urn."

"It was some of your best work, Beck," added Storm.

I nodded.

"Thanks, you guys," said Beck, her attention still on the map. "Not to brag, but I think I just topped myself. When you look at that wall through the Sacred Stone, you can see a second map filled with inscriptions.

"It's way more detailed," Beck reported. "And it looks like we're not supposed to go directly to the City of Gold. We have to take a detour first. To a temple of some sort..."

"What?" I said. "We can't take a detour. Mom and Chaupi need the gold from the lost city to stop Juan Carlos Rojas and save the rain forest."

"Well, I'm sorry, Bick. I didn't draw the map. I wasn't even born in the 1530s, which was probably when Inkarri or his friends painted the wall of this cave with their invisible ink or whatever they used to hide the real route to Paititi."

"May I take a look?" asked Storm.

"Totally," said Tommy. "And Storm? Can you memorize it?"

"Well, duh," said Storm. "It's what I do."

While Storm gazed at the map through the Sacred Stone, Beck dashed off a quick sketch of what she had seen on the wall.

"Well done, you two," said Storm, after she'd soaked up the visuals and committed them to memory. "I believe you have just discovered the final key to locating Paititi."

"This is so awesome!" said Tommy. He stuck his fingers in his mouth and let loose the family whistle. "We need to show Dad."

"But not Chet Collier," I said.

"I agree with Bick," said Beck. "And not just because we're twins. That Collier kid is sketchy."

"He doesn't need to know about the map," said Storm. "His purpose on this expedition is to document rain-forest devastation."

"And make us TV stars," added Tommy, practicing his head tilt and toothy smile. "But he doesn't need the map for that either."

He whistled again.

Dad didn't whistle back.

But somebody else did. Somebody who'd just stepped into that rectangular window of bright sunlight. Even though he was in silhouette, I recognized his ridiculous French Foreign Legion cap.

It was that jerk Guy Dubonnet Merck!

CHAPTER 48

Merck whistled again, and three armed thugs appeared.

They had their weapons trained on Dad and Chet Collier, both of whom had their hands up over their heads.

Storm, still holding the Sacred Stone, tried to hide it behind her back. It didn't work. The sunlight streaming through that rectangular opening hit the faceted rock, and it shot a dozen bright yellow dots, like a cluster of laser beams, against the walls. If we were cats, we would've chased them immediately.

"Aha!" exclaimed Merck in his thick French accent. "*Voilà!* You have done our job for us. You have found *la pierre sacrée*—the Sacred Stone!" He holstered his pistol and turned to one of his goons, a guy carrying a very long duffel bag, like you'd use for skis. "Jacques?"

"Oui?"

"It is the moment of truth. We must see if the stone fits!" Merck held out his hand to Storm. "Kindly give me the jewel, *petite fille*."

"Whoa," said Tommy, bristling. "What'd you just call my sister?"

"A little girl," said Merck.

"Oh. Okay, then. I think."

Storm looked to Dad. The goon guarding him cocked back the hammer on his rifle.

"Do as Monsieur Merck instructs," said Dad.

"And please hurry," begged Chet Collier, whose captor had just jammed a pistol into the small of his back. "These guys' trigger fingers look extremely twitchy."

Storm lobbed the Sacred Stone across the cave to Merck. He caught it one-handed, which was a good thing, because he always posed with his other hand tucked into his safari jacket, as if he were Napoleon with an eye patch.

"Now then, Jacques," he said to the heavy toting the duffel. "The staff!"

"*Oui,* Monsieur Merck!"

Jacques unzipped the bag and pulled out the golden Incan rod that Mom, Dad, and Tommy had found back on Cocos Island—the one that went with the high priest's headdress.

Merck fondled the yellow sapphire with his fingers for a few seconds and then, barely able to contain his delight, fitted it into that empty hole in the corncob at the tip of the golden staff.

"The corncob is complete!" shouted Merck. "Our friends will now be able to perform the sacred ritual and enter the Lost City of Gold."

"With a corncob?" muttered Tommy. "That's, like, so totally random."

"You're forgetting," said Storm, shifting into teacher mode, "that corn is what made the Incan Empire possible. Corn and, of course, llama poop."

"What?" said just about everybody in the cavern.

"Llama droppings were the fertilizer that allowed maize to take root high up in the Andes Mountains where it otherwise couldn't have survived," Storm explained.

We all just nodded.

And then Merck got back to business.

"The high priest will be most happy when we present him with the restored Incan rod. For this, we thank you." He kissed the air twice. "Mwah! Mwah! *Merci beaucoup!* Thank you so very much."

“Now do we get to kill them?” asked the eager goon with his gun aimed at Dad.

Merck grinned, stroked his chin, and thought about it long and hard.

Which was a good thing.

I really wasn’t in a hurry to die.

CHAPTER 49

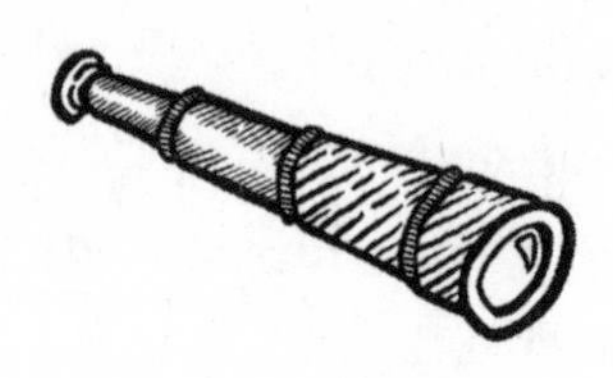

"*Non!*" Merck finally announced.

I'm pretty sure that *non* is French for "no" because the instant he said it, his grumbling goon squad lowered their weapons.

"But we have not killed anyone all day," complained Jacques.

"I know, *mon ami*," said Merck. "So, if you see a jaguar, you have my permission to shoot it. No questions asked. Just point and click. But these Kidds and their young friend, Monsieur Collier? We will let them live. For, as you see, they are always stumbling upon things that I can sell to the highest bidder. First the high priest's rod and headdress. Now the Sacred Stone. Who knows when I might need something else and so will need them to find it for me? We let them live. But only if you promise not to follow after us. Do we have a deal, Professor Dr. Kidd?"

"Oui," said Dad, who can say "yes" in French with the best of 'em. "We will not follow you. For, as you just said, you seldom know where it is you are going unless we have been there first."

"This is so very true. And so, we bid you *au revoir.* Thank you once again for finding the sacred sapphire, because I had no clue where to look. Seriously, that map?" He made an explosion noise as he flicked his fingers away from his head. "Blew my mind. Had no idea what all those dots and squiggles were all about. But thanks to you Kidds, I am becoming filthy rich. Come, my minions. We must take our treasure to the high priest who awaits us at the gates to Paititi!"

We stood there and watched them leave.

Finally, when we were sure they were long gone, Storm spoke up.

"Too bad they have no idea where they are going," she said.

"Unfortunately," Dad said with a sigh, "they might. I suspect they are working with whoever it was that stole the treasure map off the *Lost.* It would explain why Merck was on the island robbing us while the pirates were on the ship burgling us. And why he just referenced seeing the map even though he wasn't the one who stole it."

"Doesn't matter," said Beck, gesturing to the painted wall that the four of us had blocked the instant Merck and his French henchmen stepped into our cave. "They still don't know how to find Paititi."

"My goodness," said Dad. "It's the map."

"Totally," said Tommy. "But check this out—it's like that map you left for us on the *Lost* that one time."

"There's another map painted on top of it with ancient invisible ink!" I blurted out, because I get super-excited whenever I have a huge secret.

"What do you mean?" asked Collier.

"There was a detailed rendering of the precise

path to Paititi painted on top of the much more generalized treasure map!" said Beck. "That's why Father Toledo's letter made such a big deal about finding the Sacred Stone that would, and I quote, 'reveal all'!"

"Beck could see the secret map only when she looked at the wall through the Sacred Stone," I explained.

"I drew the map," said Beck.

"Did Storm see it as well?" asked Dad.

"Yes, sir," said Storm.

"Beck?"

"Yes, Dad?"

"Destroy your drawing."

"No problem." She ripped the sketch out of her sketchbook, tore it in half, and gave one scrap of paper to me. Then we both popped the paper into our mouths and chewed.

"Um, that was dumb," said Collier. "You guys gave the stone that allowed you to read the real map to Merck! Then you destroyed your only copy. Now you don't know how to get to Paititi either."

"Oh, yes, we do," said Tommy, turning to Storm. "Right, sis?"

Storm just smiled and tapped her temple.

Dad roared with laughter.

"That's my girl!" He said it so proudly and loudly, it echoed off the cavern walls. He marched across the dusty chamber and gave Storm a huge bear hug!

Then he motioned for the rest of us to join in.

Well, everybody except Chet Collier. He could do group hugs with his own family on their next televised reunion.

CHAPTER 50

We decided to make camp at the necropolis and spend the night.

It'd been a long day—complete with a three-story rock-slide ride that had left Beck and me feeling a little banged up. But thanks to the secret invisible-ink map, we were the only ones who knew the final path to Paititi, so we weren't in as huge a hurry as before.

"We'll leave at first light," Dad announced. "Your mother just advised me via a satellite-phone text that she and Chaupi have successfully stalled for time in Lima. The president and interior minister know we are very close to finding the Peruvian people's long-lost treasure. In fact, they may even want to help us. Señor Rojas is, as you might imagine, upset. He is used to getting his way and buying whatever he wants. Too bad he's never been up against a negotiator as tough as Sue Kidd or a leader as determined as Chaupi."

"Awesome," said Tommy. "I could definitely sleep. I'm totally wiped out."

"Us, too," said Beck and me.

"I am also feeling somewhat somnolent," said Storm, because it would've been way too easy for her to simply say she was drowsy.

"I'm tired, too," admitted Chet Collier with a yawn. "Exciting stuff today. Bad guys with guns. Big yellow sapphires. Golden corncobs. Secret maps painted on walls. Group hugs. I also shot some great footage of a pile of dry bones. I might be able to sell that video to the Pets Channel. They do programs that dogs like to watch."

"One last thing," said Dad, reaching into his pocket. "Before we all retire for the evening, I'd like to make a special presentation to honor you, Storm, and your big, beautiful brain. Your mother and I would like to give you a small token of our love and esteem."

He popped open the lid on a small jewelry box.

"These are your mother's favorite earrings. And she insisted that, tonight, I pass them on to you."

Dad helped Storm slip on the earrings.

Then we all crawled into our sleeping bags.

This may seem weird but, as tired as I was, I had trouble falling asleep. I guess because my brain realized that, the very next day, we would be walking into the ancient Incas' Lost City of Gold—a treasure that had eluded explorers for centuries. Thinking about that got my heart beating fast and my adrenaline pumping.

I was so stoked, I figured I'd just lie there all night staring up at the stars.

But then a mosquito bit me on the neck and I completely conked out.

At least I thought it was a mosquito.

Z-Z-Z-Z
Z-Z-Z-Z
NUMBER ONE RULE OF BLOW-DARTING? NEVER INHALE THROUGH THE STRAW!

CHAPTER 51

When we woke up the next morning (thanks to an extremely bright sun), we all had swollen welts on our necks.

Well, actually, Tommy had one on his butt.

"We were blowgunned!" I said.

"Stung by darts dipped in some kind of sleeping potion!" added Beck.

"Most likely a tropical tranquilizer," said Dad, rubbing the back of his head.

"Chya!" said Tommy, rubbing his butt. "My cheek's still numb."

And then we all waited for Storm to chime in with a more scientific, nerdy analysis of what type of knockout potion our attackers had used.

But she didn't say a word.

Because her sleeping bag was empty! Chet Collier's, too!

"They took Storm!" I shouted. "And Collier!"

"Because they figured out that Storm memorized the secret map," said Beck.

"But, um, why would they kidnap Collier?" asked Tommy. "He didn't know anything. Seriously. When it comes to knowing stuff, the guy is, like, even dumber than me."

"You're not dumb, Thomas," said Dad calmly. "And our nocturnal attackers did not kidnap Mr. Collier. In fact, I suspect that Chet Collier is the one who alerted our nefarious visitors to Storm's knowledge of the map!"

Feeling furious and frustrated, Beck and I launched into Twin Tirade number 1,105.

"I knew we shouldn't've invited Collier on this treasure hunt!" I shouted.

COLLIER'S A CREEP!
HE'S WORSE!
WHAT'S WORSE THAN A CREEP?
A BOOGER-CRUSTED CREEP!
OH, YEAH? WELL, I THINK HE'S A SLEAZY, SLIMY SCOUNDREL!
SO? I THINK HE'S A SKEEVAZOID!
WHAT'S THAT?
A WORD I JUST MADE UP.
HEY, I DO THE WORDS, YOU DO THE PICTURES!

"Yeah?" said Beck. "Well, I knew it before you, Bickford."

"Oh, really, Rebecca? Since when?"

"Since the first time he popped up out of nowhere!"

"Well, I knew it before that!"

"What?"

"I knew anybody named Collier had to be our enemy. It's, like, a rule."

"Well, it's a stupid rule. You can't jump to conclusions about people like that."

"Of course you can't," I told her. "Everybody knows that."

"So what are we arguing about?"

"I forget."

"Me, too. So we're good?" asked Beck.

"Definitely," I told her. "Except, of course, Storm is still missing. That's not good."

Dad shook his head. "All is not lost, twins. Why do you think I teamed up with young Chet yesterday?"

"Um, because he needed adult supervision?" said Tommy.

"Good point," said Dad. "But in truth, I was shadowing Chet because your mother and I have been suspicious of young Mr. Collier ever since he mysteriously showed up in the Port of Pisco right after we spotted the pirates' submarine."

Tommy snapped his fingers. "Nathan Collier has a submarine!" he said. "He used it against us in our very first treasure-hunting adventure without you and Mom."

"Collier has a whole fleet of submarines, Tommy," said Dad. "Different sizes for different purposes."

"So, um, why did you guys invite Chet along if you knew he was a spy?" I asked.

"Quite simple, Bick: Your mother and I used to be spies. One of the best tricks in the spy-craft toolbox is to keep your friends close and your enemies closer."

"Plus he had that awesome video camera to document all the rain-forest destruction and make us TV stars," said Tommy. "Guess that's not going to happen. Bummer."

"We'll worry about that later," said Dad. "Now

we need to track Storm and make sure no harm comes her way."

"Sounds like a plan," said Beck. "And how, exactly, are we going to do that?"

Dad pulled a flat gadget out of his pocket.

It was beeping. On its screen, I could see a blinking red dot. It was moving slowly across a map grid.

"With this," he said.

CHAPTER 52

Those earrings Dad gave Storm?

There was a reason they were Mom's favorites. They were actually another set of CIA-style spy gear—a pair of high-tech GPS devices that sent up a signal to a satellite, which bounced the wearer's location back down to Dad's palm-size tracking device!

"As I said, your mother and I had our suspicions about Mr. Collier all along," Dad told us as we hiked off into the jungle along the route Storm was taking, according to the steadily beeping tracker. "After I, somewhat foolishly in retrospect, congratulated Storm for memorizing the hidden map, I knew I needed to find a way to ensure her safety."

"That was smart," I said.

"Perhaps," said Dad. "But alerting Collier to Storm's secret knowledge of the precise location of Paititi was extremely dumb on my part. Perhaps the dumbest thing I have ever done. If anything happens to Stephanie, I will never forgive myself."

"Well," said Tommy, "they're not going to, you know, kill her. They need her photographic memory if they want the map. If she's dead, her big brain will probably stop working!"

It was an obvious point, of course, but a good one. The bad guys wouldn't hurt Storm, not as long as she took them where they wanted to go.

"Still," said Dad, "I am very glad that your mother insisted that I take extra precautions to safeguard Storm. She's the one who suggested I buy some insurance with the tracker earrings. If anything were to happen to Storm..."

He did not finish that thought. It was too sad to consider.

Beck looked at the flashing blip on Dad's device. "She's not going straight to Paititi," she said. "She's going to the temple first."

"The secret cave map said you had to go to the temple before going to Paititi," I explained to Tommy and Dad. "Tomb to temple to pyramid of gold."

"Any reason why?" asked Dad.

"Yes," said Beck, who had seen the map's secrets when she peered through the Sacred

Stone at the painted cave wall. “But, um, it was kind of written in Incan, so I’m not exactly sure what that reason is.”

“Storm will know,” I said.

“Totally,” added Tommy. “She can probably even read Incan.”

“Indeed,” said Dad. “When your sister was just a toddler, your mother and I gave her an ancient-languages alphabet book for her birthday. She liked it much better than the letter songs on *Sesame Street.*”

According to Dad’s tracking device, Storm was only about a mile ahead of us. She and whoever was forcing her to march through the jungle were moving slowly. Very, very slowly.

“She’s buying us time,” said Dad. “Good girl. We should catch up with Storm and her captors within the hour.”

Things were looking good.

Until we came to a clearing and had to quickly take cover behind the nearest stand of ferns.

CHAPTER 53

Remember those three angry old men dressed in traditional Quechuan costumes we'd bumped into back at Qurikancha, the Incan temple in Cuzco?

Well, we'd bumped into them again. They were fifteen yards in front of us and they weren't alone. They were standing with a pack of young warriors, all of them decked out in what looked like the kind of clothes ancient Incan warriors would've worn when they battled the Spanish conquistadors way back in the 1500s.

Several of the young guys were holding long

blowguns. I had to figure they were the ones who'd nailed us with their tranquilizer darts the night before.

One of the older guys was wearing the high priest's headdress Merck had stolen from us on Cocos Island. He was also holding the golden staff (which Merck had also stolen) with the yellow sapphire (which Merck had stolen most recently) mounted on top in the corncob.

Now it seemed that these angry guys had stolen it all from Merck! Because they had him and his three French henchmen trapped and suspended in a hunting net.

"Mr. Collier tells us he no longer needs you, Guy Dubonnet Merck!" decreed the elderly man wearing the high priest's headdress and holding the golden staff with the sparkling jewel in its tip. "He says you have found everything we shall require to perform the sacred ritual."

"Everything, that is, except for that which is most important," added the spookiest-looking old man in the group. "A human heart to offer to Inti, the god of the sun!"

"Sacré bleu!" shouted Merck, trapped in the net. "Nathan Collier and I had a deal."

"This is a very high honor, Mr. Merck," said another one of the elders. "Those of us in this cult seek to revive the ancient powers of the Incas. To fulfill our destiny, we must offer a human sacrifice. You will be our messenger to the supreme sun god!"

“Can’t you just send him a text?” squealed Merck. “Maybe an e-mail?”

“Do not mock the all-powerful, almighty, and most benevolent Inti!” cried the priest. “Prepare your soul for its journey to the sun!”

Wow. They were really going to do this. The crazy cult dudes were going to slay Guy Dubonnet Merck.

CHAPTER 54

"Finally," said the cult member dressed in the priest costume, "thanks to our rich and powerful new friend, we have everything we need to find Inkarri's Lost City of Gold."

His warriors rattled their blowguns.

The fanatical leader raised his arms toward the sky. "We have the ancient staff and ceremonial headpiece of the Willaq Umu, the high priest of the sun. We have the girl with the hidden map written inside her memory."

"Really?" said Merck. "I don't see her. Maybe

you should cut me down so I can help you recapture her."

"She is with the Colliers," said the cult guy in a wool hat. "At the temple."

"There they will learn what I must say to raise Paititi!" said the cult's priest. "What words I, the high priest of the sun, must say when we offer Inti the ancient sacrifice that he demands—your still-beating heart. Prepare to die!"

"All of us?" cried one of Merck's goons.

"No," said the priest. "Just your chief. He who hides one eye."

"Silence!" the cult leader shouted at Merck's cronies, who were celebrating the fact that they wouldn't have their hearts removed. "Supay?"

One of the big guys toting a blowgun fell to his knees. "Yes, Your High Holiness?"

"Prepare the sacrificial *tumi*. Make certain its blade is sharp so it might cut clean!"

"Yes, Your High Holiness!" Supay ran off.

I wiped some sweat out of my eyes and wondered, *What will these guys do to Storm after she takes them where they want to go?*

"We're in luck," I heard Dad whisper to Tommy.

"Um, how's that?" Tommy whispered back.

Dad wiggled his satellite phone. "I did some quick research online. Today is definitely our lucky day! We just have to wait a few more minutes."

"They're going to kill Merck," I said.

"No. We are going to stop them." Dad checked his dive watch. "We just have to wait fourteen minutes and thirty-two seconds."

So that's what we did.

We kept still.

We remained quiet.

We waited fourteen minutes and thirty-two seconds.

CHAPTER 55

Time seemed to slow down.

The only sounds in that clearing were Merck whimpering, the buzzing of bugs, some birds cawing, and the distant scrape of stone against steel as the warrior Supay sharpened the edge of his deadly blade.

"Stay put," said Dad when fourteen minutes and thirty-two seconds were finally up. He handed his tracker device and satellite phone to Tommy. "I'm going to borrow a page from Mark Twain's *A Connecticut Yankee in King Arthur's Court.*"

"Huh?" I said.

"Remind me to ask your mother to add that classic to your American literature reading list

ASAP. Now then, Thomas, if this doesn't go the way I'm hoping it will, you're in charge. Go rescue your sister."

"B-b-but—" stammered Tommy.

"That's an order."

Tommy nodded. "Okay. But be careful out there."

Dad gave us all a smile and a wink. "Don't worry. I have science and, of course, the moon on my side."

None of us had any idea what the heck he was talking about.

Dad stood up and spread open the wall of ferns he'd been hiding behind. He boldly stepped into the jungle clearing.

"Begone from this place!" he bellowed.

The priest and his army spun around to see who would dare interrupt their sacred ritual.

"Infidel!" shouted the guy in the priest costume. "Intruder!"

His young warriors raised their primitive weapons and aimed them at Dad.

"You dare to raise your weapons at me?" Dad

growled. He sounded like the mighty Mufasa from that movie *The Lion King*. Yes, I have a personal DVD player on board the *Lost* and I'm not afraid to use it. "Very well! Because you dare to threaten me, you leave me no choice. I must take the sun from the sky!"

He raised his arms.

"Begone, sun! May the moon smother you whole!"

The puzzled priest looked up to the sky and gasped.

The sun was starting to disappear behind a round shadow. It was going dark, blocked out by the moon.

"No!" cried the priest. "You cannot do this thing!"

Dad laughed his best diabolical-supervillain laugh. "I'm doing it, aren't I?"

I grabbed the satellite phone from Tommy to do a quick search. I tapped in the words *solar* and *eclipse.*

Yep. Just as I suspected.

That was the science Dad had known was on our side. This was definitely our lucky day because it was the first total solar eclipse in this part of Peru in fourteen years, and it happened exactly when we needed it to. Well, we had to wait those fourteen minutes and thirty-two seconds, but, come on, that's still pretty lucky.

"Give us back the sun!" shouted the priest. "Restore Inti!"

"Only if you release your captives and leave this place! Now!"

I was kind of hoping Dad would also ask the

high priest to give back his rod, the Sacred Stone, and his headgear, but I could tell Dad didn't want to press his luck, even though this was our super-lucky day.

The priest hesitated. He looked at the net with his squirming prisoners. He looked to the sky. The sun was slowly disappearing behind a shadow.

"Cut them down!" he ordered.

One of the young warriors sliced a rope with his knife. Merck and his trapped buddies tumbled to the ground in a jumbled ball.

"Flee!" Dad shouted to the Incan wannabes. Overhead, the sun grew even darker.

"You have not freed the sun!" shouted the withered old guy in the hat.

"And I will not until I know that you and your men are long gone from this place!"

Dad knew a total solar eclipse would last about two hours. Even he couldn't rush it.

"Flee now, or I swear by Viracocha, I will extinguish the sun forever!"

Finally, they all fled. Fast!

When he was absolutely certain they were

gone, Dad signaled for us to come out from our hiding places. The four of us marched over to where Merck and his thugs lay in a heap on the ground, still tangled up in that hunting net.

"*Merci beaucoup,* Dr. Kidd," said Merck, grinning up at us even though his face was mushed in a mesh of rope. "We are most grateful that you rescued us. Now, if you will kindly cut us out of this netting."

Dad shook his head.

"Not until you answer a few questions."

"Very well. We are, as you say, in your debt."

"Did Nathan Collier hire you to steal the Incan headpiece and rod from us on Cocos?"

"Oui," said Merck.

"And the Sacred Stone?"

"*Oui.* This was also Monsieur Collier, aided, of course, by his scoundrel of a son Chet, who has a, how you say, satellite phone. He also suggested to his father that he should have these crazed cultists kidnap your daughter and bring her to him. Apparently the one you call Storm is the only one who knows precisely where to find the Lost City of Paititi, *non?*"

Dad didn't answer. Instead, he asked a question of his own.

"An undertaking of this magnitude would prove quite expensive. Tell me: Who's funding Nathan Collier?"

"Easy," said Merck. "Juan Carlos Rojas!"

CHAPTER 56

Dad sliced through the net with his enormous knife.

Seriously. The thing is the size of Pinocchio's nose when he's been fibbing.

Guy Dubonnet Merck and his men spilled out of their tangled trap like limes out of a bag with a hole in the bottom.

"*Merci,* Dr. Kidd. *Merci,*" said Merck as he creaked up from the ground on wobbly legs and dusted off his khaki riding pants. "Has anyone seen my hat?"

One of his henchmen handed Merck his French Foreign Legion cap.

"Somehow, it ended up in my shoe, *mon ami,*"

the guy said. *"Je suis désolé."*

"You should be sorry!" said Merck, slapping the flapped hat against his arm to air it out. "Now it smells like *fromage!*"

That's when I really missed Storm. She would've told me *fromage* meant "cheese."

Beck and I had already done a quick survey of the scene. When the high priest and his cult buddies took off, they'd grabbed all of Merck's crew's weapons. Of course, all we had was Dad's hunting knife.

Did I mention the thing is ginormous?

Advantage Kidd Family.

"Before we let you and your assorted thugs leave this rain forest—*forever,*" said Dad, seething with rage, "we need to know everything you know."

"Why?" asked Merck. "I was a very bad student in school. I almost flunked French, and I am, how you say, French."

"The only information I require from you, Monsieur Merck, has to do with my daughter Storm." Dad's temper was flaring hotter than a meteor that had just hit Earth's atmosphere.

(I wonder if Beck and I got our amazing Twin Tirade talents from Dad.)

"Where did they take her?" Dad demanded.

"To the temple that she saw on the secret map," said Merck quickly.

Dad's face was maybe an inch from Merck's. The knife? It was pretty close to the skeevy guy's scrawny neck.

Merck spilled everything he knew as fast as he could. "The man in the headdress, the nasty gentleman who was going to cut out my heart and offer it to the sun god first thing tomorrow morning, he knows your daughter can take him and his followers the 'final distance' to the Lost City of Gold. Juan Carlos Rojas has given these cuckoo birds who call themselves the New Incas everything they need to reclaim the treasure and glory of their vanquished ancestors—your daughter with the map in her head, the jeweled staff, the sacred headpiece, and, of course, the brilliant archaeologist Nathan Collier!"

"Excuse me?" said Tommy, chuffing a laugh. "Who told them that Collier was brilliant?"

"The guy's totally lame," said Beck.

"He couldn't find a watermelon in a washtub," I said. "Once, Nathan Collier saw a sign that said 'Disneyland, Left,' so he turned around and went home."

I could've gone on snapping Collier all day.

But Dad was glaring at me.

CHAPTER 57

"Bick?" said Dad, shaking his head. "Too much?"

"Little bit," said Tommy.

"We're kind of in a hurry to rescue Storm," added Beck.

"Right. Gotcha. My bad," I said sheepishly. Collier is just such an easy target!

"Monsieur Merck?" Dad said, lowering his knife, because the guy was cooperating. Merck was also shaking like a shirt hanging on a clothesline in a hurricane. "Please go on.

Tell us everything you know. Don't leave anything out."

"Very well. Nathan Collier and his men have been trailing you on *motocyclettes,* what you call ATVs—all-terrain vehicles."

Beck and I nodded. "We're familiar with ATVs."

"Très bon," said Merck. "His son, the greasy one they call Chet, was wearing a GPS tracking device the whole time that he was traveling with you."

"Was the GPS tracker in a pair of earrings?" asked Tommy.

"No," said Merck. "I believe the transmitter is hidden in what they call a high-school class ring?"

The one that Chet was always twisting and nervously fiddling with!

"Go on," said Dad.

"Nathan Collier and now his son have solemnly sworn to the Incan cult's priest that they alone know all the magic words that must be recited for the city of Paititi to rise up from its hiding place."

"Whoa," said Tommy. "The Lost City of Gold is underground?"

"*Oui*. This is what Nathan Collier has told the members of this strange and mystical sect. And only he knows the sacred ritual to make it reappear. And when it does, when Collier—who, as you may recall from my earlier confession, is being paid by Juan Carlos Rojas—gives these New Incas the gold that their ancestors hid from the conquistadors five centuries ago, they will give the rain forest to Rojas!"

Dad still had an extremely stern look on his face.

"This sacred ritual," he said, "it involves a human sacrifice?"

"*Oui.* Many ancient Incan rites did. So the new high priest needs to do it, too. That was why they were going to slice me open and remove my still-beating heart from my rib cage and why I am so grateful to you, Professor Thomas Kidd, for rescuing me. Mwah! Mwah! I kiss you tenderly upon both of your cheeks. Mwah! Mwah! I do it again."

Dad just stood there and took the kisses. From the look in his eyes, his mind was a million miles away in a place that wasn't very cheerful.

"So," said Tommy, "if they don't have your human heart, game over. No golden city rising up from the jungle floor."

"Unless," said Dad grimly, his mind snapping back from whatever dark world it had just visited, "they've already found a replacement."

"Oui," said Merck. "And these strange New Incas, they love child sacrifices."

The answer hit us.

"Storm!"

CHAPTER 58

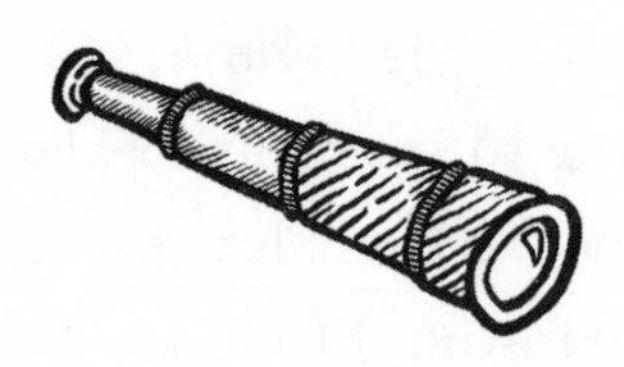

Dad sent Merck packing.

He was extremely eager to go.

"By this time tomorrow, I will be in Marseilles, nibbling on chocolate croissants and drinking bouillabaisse through a straw!"

Beck urped. "Isn't bouillabaisse a fish stew?"

"Oui."

Beck urped again. Me, too. How do you suck floating fish chunks through a straw?

"*Au revoir,* Kidd Family Treasure Hunters." Merck saluted us. "*Merci beaucoup,* once again, for saving my life. I hope you are able to also save the life of the one you call Storm."

Merck and his men hurried to a pile of lush

green vines that was actually a camouflage canopy hiding a helicopter. They got in and took off.

"There are ATV tread marks over in the muddy banks of that river," said Dad, pointing east. He checked his GPS tracker. "We may not have Storm and her memorized treasure map but we have her coordinates. We also have a very easy trail to follow because Nathan Collier always prefers to ride instead of hike."

"Too true," said Tommy. "If he hiked, he might sweat."

"And," I said, "if he sweats, his forehead hair curl might come unglued."

Collier, who was about as short as me (he always made sure he was photographed standing on a box) was famous on cable TV for his dashing "Look at Me, I'm an Explorer" costume: dusty boots (even if he was nowhere near a desert), khaki pants, khaki shirt, faded leather bomber jacket, and a jaunty captain's hat. His hair was always perfectly coiffed, with one curl dangling just above his left eyebrow. I think he used Elmer's Glue for hair gel.

We had followed the banks of the swollen river

for maybe half a mile when, all of a sudden, we heard a scream.

"Help us!" cried a woman. "The snake! It wants my baby!"

Dad and Tommy took off running.

Beck and I were right behind them.

We rounded a bend in the river.

I couldn't believe what I saw: A giant anaconda! A monster snake, seventeen feet long!

It was slithering toward a woman shielding a little girl, probably her daughter, on the riverbank.

Just in case you don't read as many cheesy books or watch as many "Eaten Alive!" clips on YouTube as I sometimes do when we're on board the *Lost* and I've finished all my homework, let me fill you in on a few anaconda details.

One: They're huge. Officially, the anaconda is the largest snake in the whole world.

Two: They're basically at the top of the food chain in the Amazon.

Three: They're not poisonous. They don't have to be! An anaconda waits for its prey to come down to the water's edge, strikes fast, coils its body around its victim, and squeezes until it crushes the life out of its target. Also, an anaconda can unhinge its jaw to swallow large prey whole.

The good news? Once an anaconda wolfs down, say, an entire mammal, it won't be hungry for a few months.

Now it was all set to snack on two.

Unless we stopped it, this snake might not have to eat again for half a year!

At that point, Tommy bravely (or maybe stupidly) grabbed hold of a vine and swung into action!

CHAPTER 59

Tommy went flying, Tarzan-style, through the underbrush.

"Careful, son!" shouted Dad.

"Don't worry!" cried Tommy. "I remember all those anti-snake self-defense tactics you taught me when I was in kindergarten!"

Tommy didn't rush up to the head of the snake. Instead, he made a pretty surprising move.

He grabbed the giant snake's tail, raised the tip to his mouth, and chomped down.

Gross.

When Tommy's teeth sank into that pointy tip, I could've sworn I heard the snake yelp the way a dog does when you accidentally step on its tail.

"The tip of the tail is the most sensitive part of the giant snake's body," Dad proudly explained as we watched the monster reptile slither back into the river.

"Thank you!" said the breathless woman, still shielding her scared child. "You saved my daughter."

"No problem," said Tommy, spitting out some flecks of snake scales. "Happy to help."

"You are very brave and heroic," said the woman.

"And, not for nothing, *you* speak excellent English."

"Gracias," said the woman. "Spanish, too."

"Because I am the leader of this tribe and she is my wife," said a man who stepped out of the thick foliage. "Education is a very important priority for me and my family."

Judging by his purple-and-yellow-feathered headgear and elaborate jewelry, the man who had just joined us along the riverbank was probably some kind of royalty in this neck of the rain forest. Two golden medallions were glittering on the leather necklace dangling on his chest. They reminded me of the amulets Beck and I had picked up when we saved that other chief's son in the flood.

"Education is very important in our family also," said Dad, extending his hand, which the local royal took. "That's why Tommy knew how to defeat the anaconda."

"Chya," said Tommy. "Snake Attack 101. I totally did my homework for that class. You goof up on the final exam, there's no such thing as a do-over."

"You are most courageous," said the grateful chief. "Much braver than the American explorers who came this way yesterday on roaring horses that snorted smoke from their tails."

I think he meant Nathan Collier and his crew on the gas-guzzling ATVs.

"When they saw my wife and child on the banks of the river, about to be attacked by the monster snake, they did not pass the test. They did nothing."

"The giant anaconda was here yesterday?" asked Beck.

The chief nodded. "But worry not. My wife and child were never really in danger. We have trained the snake to do our bidding."

"No way!" said Tommy.

"Way," said the chief. "It is all part of an ancient character test to help us choose the most deserving explorer, for we have long known that this moment would one day come."

"Um, what moment are we talking about?" I asked.

He glanced at the medallion on my necklace

and smiled. "When Inkarri would be made whole and Paititi would rise from its hiding place."

I wasn't exactly sure what that had to do with a fake snake attack, but I nodded like I did. The chief had a very spooky way of saying things. He raised his necklace over his head and presented his two golden charms to Tommy.

"Good luck with your quest," he said.

Tommy bowed slightly as the chief draped the pair of medals over his head.

"You have earned your reward. May Inkarri protect and assist you."

I checked out Tommy's new swag. His pair of golden ornaments looked a lot like the two legs Beck and I were still wearing around our necks. Somehow, I didn't think that was a coincidence.

CHAPTER 60

The chief lent us a guide to assist us on the last leg of our journey.

"She will make certain that you find the ancient Incan temple you speak of," he told us. "She knows its location well."

"She?" said Tommy.

"My oldest daughter."

"We appreciate the offer," said Dad, "but—"

"But nothing!" said Tommy.

Because the chief's oldest daughter had just stepped out of the rain forest and into a golden beam of sunlight. Even I knew she was gorgeous. Believe it or not, Mattel makes a Princess of the

Incas Barbie Doll. I think the chief's daughter, whose name was Milagros, might've been the model. She seemed to be the same age as Tommy, so of course he tail-spun into love immediately.

With Milagros in the lead, we left the river trail and took a different one.

"This way will be much faster," she said. "It is an old jaguar path. We will find your missing daughter much sooner if we follow it."

"So," said Tommy after we'd hiked maybe another mile, "are you, like, a princess?"

"Yes," said Milagros. "Because I am a princess."

"Cool. Is there a prince?"

"Yes," said Milagros. "That is what my brother has named his dog."

As we trekked through the steamy jungle, Dad made satellite-phone contact with Mom.

"Nathan Collier and his people, including his despicable son Chet, have kidnapped Storm," he told her. "Juan Carlos Rojas hired Collier and his team to help him find the Lost City of Paititi. Rojas has promised the gold to the leaders of an Incan cult. They, in exchange, have promised Rojas all the rain-forest trees he desires."

"Something they do not own," said Mom's voice through the speakerphone.

"True," said Dad. "But if they have all the gold..."

"Then we don't," said Mom. We could hear her sigh all the way from Lima.

"And if you and Chaupi don't back up your plea for the rain forest with an incredible treasure..." said Dad.

"It will fall on deaf ears in the presidential palace," said Mom.

It's true; Mom and Dad are so in sync, they often finish each other's sentences like that.

"The negotiations have hit a roadblock," said Mom. "Señor Rojas seemed pretty pleased with himself, and now I know why."

"Probably because Nathan Collier and his crew are very close to finding the Lost City of Paititi."

"Well," said Mom, "we can't let Collier beat us to the treasure this time. If he does, Rojas wins. And if Rojas wins, he'll chainsaw and torch his initials into more acres of rain forest. I'm coming there to help you, Thomas."

"Good," said Dad. "And tell Chaupi to bring the cavalry. We might need major reinforcements. I feel confident that Rojas has hired a sizable army."

"Thomas?"

"Yes?"

"Be careful."

"We always are," said Dad, conveniently not mentioning Tommy, the giant anaconda, or Collier's plan to perform an ancient Incan child-sacrifice ritual with Storm's still-beating heart.

"Follow Storm's GPS tracker when you and Chaupi are airborne," said Dad. "Have your chopper set down wherever she might be. We plan on being right there with her!"

"Will do. Love you guys. Can't wait until we're all together again."

I felt the same way.

I couldn't wait until our whole family was one happy unit.

Because that would mean we'd rescued Storm!

CHAPTER 61

With Milagros's expert knowledge of the jungle, we came to a secluded rise above the vine-choked ruins of what had once been a major Incan temple.

The temple wasn't much. Just a stone altar set in front of a wall of stacked boulders that glowed like an angry face in the orangish twilight of the setting sun. Nathan and Chet Collier and maybe six other goons, their ATVs parked off to the side, stood in a circle with our old friend the cult's high priest and his knife-wielding buddy Supay.

They were surrounding the stone table in the center of the clearing.

The ancient Incan altar where Storm lay!

But the sacrifice hadn't started. Storm was just being Storm.

"I need to sack out," she said with a yawn, stretching out on the stone slab. "Exhausting couple of days. Next time, you guys should bring a spare ATV so your prisoner doesn't have to walk!"

"Why did you lead us to these ruins?" demanded Collier.

"Because that's what the secret map said to do."

"But why?"

"I don't know. Maybe so you could cleanse your spirit before you press on to Paititi. I know you should definitely cleanse your shorts. I can smell them way over here—"

"Silence!" decreed the phony priest, who was all decked out in full Incan garb. He was carrying that golden corncob staff like the drum major in a marching band. "Watch your tongue, for this is your final night on earth. Tomorrow, as the sun rises, your heart will be offered to Inti, the god of the sun!"

"Um, not to rain all over your delusional parade," said Storm, feisty as ever, "but if I remember correctly—and I always do—to re-create the sacrificial rite of *capacocha,* you need a child chosen for his or her perfection, not just the first kid you grabbed in a blowgun raid. I'm pretty sure your sun god is looking for someone who, according to everything I've memorized, is healthy, strong, beautiful, and pure. Well, I'm coming down with a cold. Either that or I'm allergic to torture. I'm also not very strong. In fact, I'm probably the weakest member of my family. And, yes, I am beautiful, but not in what you'd call the traditional sense. As for purity? Let's be honest, guys. The only thing I know that's pure is a bar of floating soap—"

"Silence!" shouted the high priest again.

"Knock it off," said Nathan Collier.

"You'll have to do," added his son. "Sorry. You're the only child we've got."

The two Incas eyeballed Chet.

"Whoa. Back off. I turned eighteen on my last birthday."

"Whatever," said Storm. "Now, like I said, if I'm going to be your big important sacrifice, I need to get my beauty rest."

"Fine!" said Collier. "But in the morning you will take us to the gates of Paititi!"

"No," whispered Dad from our hidden listening post. "Storm's not taking them anywhere."

"Why not?" asked Tommy.

"Because we're going to rescue her!"

CHAPTER 62

Dad turned to Milagros.

"Thank you for bringing us this far. Now you should go home to your family."

"But—"

"What we are about to do won't be safe. This mission is for us Kidds to undertake. I can't ask you to risk your life to help save my family."

"Why not?" said Milagros. "Didn't your son risk himself to save my mother and little sister?"

"True," said Tommy, puffing up his chest. "I did do that. Kind of bravely and heroically, as I recall."

"With a trained snake," said Beck, shooting him down.

"Maybe," said Tommy. "But I didn't know it was, you know, a fake snake at the time. All I saw was danger. And, of course, the giant anaconda, because, hey, it'd be hard not to see a snake that big—"

"What's up with the character test anyway?" I asked.

"Father senses the moment for Inkarri to return grows near," explained Milagros. "This is something our people have been anticipating for a very long time. The golden amulets Tommy now wears around his neck have been in our village for centuries."

"What do the two things have to do with each other?" I asked.

"I do not know," said Milagros. "I don't even know why my father gifted them to you."

"I think he digs me," said Tommy.

"Children?" said Dad. "Time is wasting. Please, Milagros. Return to your home. Thank your father for his extraordinary gifts."

"Including you," said Tommy with a wink. Then he made a thumb-and-pinkie-finger phone that he wiggled next to his ear as he mouthed, *Call me.*

Milagros mouthed back, *Can't. We don't own a phone.*

Anyway, as the sun sank slowly in the west, Tommy and his latest girlfriend said good-bye.

As soon as Milagros left and the sky filled with stars, Dad gave us our assignments.

"We need to split up once again," he said. "Here's the battle plan. When the guards sit down to dinner, we make our move. Tommy, you swing to the right. Cause a distraction."

Tommy nodded. "I could kick-start their ATVs."

"Excellent idea. The noise will draw them away from the altar. Hopefully, one or more of their security personnel will abandon their weapons as they dash off to see what all the noise is about."

"So you'll be able to snag a rifle!" said Tommy.

Dad nodded. "I'll take as many as I can."

"What do we do?" asked Beck.

"You and Bick grab your sister. If you spy any weapons, grab those, too. Then hightail it back up here. This will be our rendezvous spot. It's a very defensible position."

"So, um, this battle plan," I said. "It's for a real battle?"

"Yes, Bick," said Dad. "And it's a battle we need to win!"

I gulped a little.

And wished Mom had already arrived with whatever kind of cavalry she and Chaupi could muster!

CHAPTER 63

We crept down the hill as stealthily as possible.

I froze when my foot hit a loose rock that sent a shower of pebbles skittering down the slope.

A couple of the guys with guns, sitting on the ground not too far from where Storm snoozed on top of the altar, looked up from their tin dinner plates.

"Did you hear that?" said one.

"Probably just some giant insect," said another. "Or a tree frog."

“That sounded more like a rock than a tree frog,” said the first guy.

“Okay. Fine,” said the other one. “Then it’s a rock frog. Now, if you don’t mind, I’m starving here.”

The paramilitary types went back to chowing down on whatever slop Nathan Collier’s Treasure Extractors Inc. had provided for their evening meal. Whatever it was, it involved some serious slurping.

Nathan Collier, his son Chet, the high priest, and the guy called Supay were back at the rocks, studying a map. Six yards away, leaning up against the craggy back wall of borders, were all the security troops’ rifles, neatly leaning against one another like the poles of a tepee.

Very convenient.

We skulked closer to the altar. So close, we could hear Storm snoring. By the way, they were totally fake snores. Storm is the worst actress in our whole family.

Off to our right, we heard the *ker-pow*

blatt-blatt-blatt of a four-stroke engine on a quad sputtering to life. Tommy must've goosed the throttle, too, because next we heard a peppy *whine-a-chug-chug.* A second ATV roared to life. Then a third. I figured Tommy must be dancing around kick-starting them all.

"Someone's stealing our rides, man!" screamed one of the goons.

"Seize them!" shouted Collier.

"Bring them to me!" cried the high priest. "They will pay for their insolence!"

Just like we had hoped, Collier's whole gang ran off to chase down the ATV thieves—forgetting their weapons in the process.

Beck and I ran to Storm as Dad ran to the stack of rifles. Once he had one in each hand, he dashed over to the ATVs to help Tommy.

Storm shot out her arms and legs, splaying them across the altar. But she didn't jump off the high stone table.

"Get up!" I shouted at Storm. "It's time to go!"

"No," said Storm. "Not until they're all gone!"

GO AWAY, GUYS. I'M SLEEPING.
HEY!
CHUG-PUTTA-CHUG

"What?" said Beck. "Don't be ridiculous."

"I'm not budging from this altar!" Storm protested.

She locked her fingers around the rough edge of the stone slab and wouldn't let go!

CHAPTER 64

"Are you crazy?" I hollered. "Let go of the stone."

"Get off the altar, Storm," added Beck. "Hurry!"

"No! I need to stay here."

"No," said Beck, "you need to come with us."

"You don't understand," said Storm.

"Yes, we do," I said. "You're stubborn. Like a mule in molasses!"

While we argued, ATVs were revving all around us. People were shouting and running around wildly. Dad was calling Tommy's name. It was basically bedlam.

"Storm," I said, "we don't have time for this! Beck?"

She nodded. "On three!"

"One...two...three!"

We both shoved with all our might and rolled Storm off the slab.

When we did, we realized why she had been so eager to stay on the altar.

There was a map carved into the stone tabletop.

A map that showed a direct route from the ancient temple to a symbol that—uh-oh—probably represented the hidden location of the Lost City of Gold.

Oops.

I heard the roar of an approaching trail bike. A blinding light seared our eyes. Several times.

It was Nathan Collier. On an ATV. Grinning like crazy. He had just used his phone to take several flash photos of the slab map.

"Aha!" cried Collier. "Another ancient symbol for Inkarri! The final route to Paititi has been revealed. No wonder your secret map sent you here first, Stephanie."

"Don't call me—"

Collier cut her off with a pistol point.

"Thank you once again, Kidd Family Treasure

Hunters! You have shown me the way. Good-bye, Stephanie and other assorted Kidd children. You are all free to go. We won't be needing any of you anymore! The gold is mine! All mine!"

He roared off on his ATV. Chet and the hired heavies followed after him. So did the high priest and Supay, the sacred-knife guy. They both hitched rides on the backs of the security goons' bikes.

Far off, I heard a rifle shot. Then another.

A few seconds later, Dad came charging back to the altar, smelling like gunpowder.

He was the one who had fired the shots.

"I missed," he said. "I was aiming for their tires. They got away. All of them."

"It doesn't matter," I said. "We have Storm!"

Dad shook his head. "But they have Tommy."

CHAPTER 65

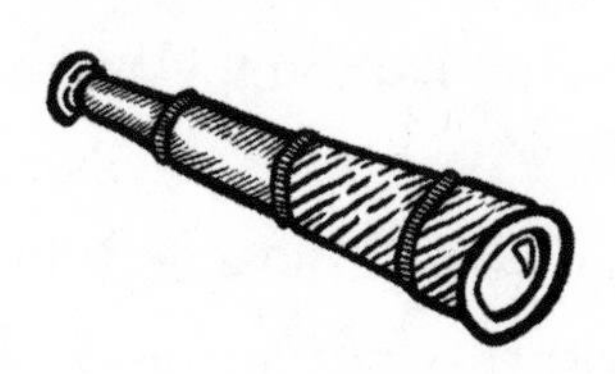

"We should go after them!" I said, tapping the top of the stone table. "We know exactly where they're headed."

"We can't leave," said Storm. "Not yet."

"Wha-hut?" said Beck. "The bad guys just kidnapped Tommy."

"They also know how to find Paititi!" I added. "Collier saw the map etched right here in the stone!" This time I pounded my fist on the altar table. Bad idea. Like I said, it was made out of stone.

"We need to move expeditiously, Storm," said Dad. "They have motorized vehicles. We do not."

“We also don’t have the one thing the secret map sent us here for,” insisted Storm.

“Yes, we do,” I said. “You can take a mental picture of the map carving. Compare it to the one you saw on the cave wall.”

“You mean when I looked through the Sacred Stone?” said Storm. She was sort of smirking, like she knew something I didn’t, which, by the way, happens on a regular basis. Storm always knows something other people don’t. Constantly.

“What are you hinting at, Stephanie?” said Dad, sounding semi-peeved. “Collier has Tommy, and, most likely, they intend to use him instead of you as the heart donor in the sacrificial rite of *capacocha*.”

Storm nodded. “He’s a way better choice. Brave. Strong—”

“Storm?” said Dad.

She took a deep breath. “You might recall that when I looked through the Sacred Stone at the cave wall, in addition to the map, I saw a verse of poetry written in the ancient alphabet of the Incas.”

"What did it say?" I asked. As the writer in the family, I guess I'm the one most interested in poetry. Except Tommy. He likes those "Roses are red" poems. Recites them to his girlfriends all the time. They usually groan when he does.

Storm gave us her translation of the ancient verse: "'At the temple near the river, within a table where hearts do quiver, you will find the final key, the secret to raising Paititi.'"

"The 'table where hearts do quiver' has to be the altar!" I said, using everything Mom taught us in our Interpretation of Poetry class.

"And 'within' has to mean 'inside'!" added Beck, because her talents are way more visual than verbal.

(Fine. Beck says my breath is extremely visual, too, especially when I'm being verbal. Look for stink lines and gas clouds in the next illustration.)

Beck and I ran our hands along the stone table, feeling for a loose stone or large seam.

"Here it is!" I called out.

"Does anybody have a screwdriver or something?" said Beck. "We need to pry it out."

"How about a bayonet?" asked Dad.

"Perfect!" said Beck.

"It'll help us scare off some of these fuzzy spiders, too!" I added.

Dad removed the bayonet from the rifle he was carrying and handed it to Beck. She used it to shoo away the spiders and wedge out the slightly tarnished golden rectangle we had discovered inside the bottom of the altar.

Speaking of bottoms, that's what seemed to be carved into the piece we'd just found.

I gave it to Storm.

"You earned it, sis," I said.

"Thanks," she said with a smile, putting the golden belly in a pocket of her cargo shorts.

"Now we all have gold medals," joked Beck. "You, me, Bick, and Tommy."

When she said that, we all dropped our heads.

"Poor Tommy." We almost whimpered it.

"Chins up, Kidds!" said Dad. "If we're lucky, they won't hurt your big brother until sunrise, when they perform their sacred rites."

"But they probably need the golden piece we just yanked out of the stone," I said.

"Well, we're not giving it to them!" said Beck.

Dad was focused on the carved map. "If I'm reading this correctly, Paititi is less than five kilometers away. An easy walk. Are you guys up for a family hike?"

"Yes, sir!" we all replied. Because this was the hike we needed to take to put our family back together.

And so we took off.

Into the jungle.

In the dark.

CHAPTER 66

We hiked the five kilometers and found another excellent hiding place on a craggy cliff high above a secluded lake. We would have stopped to admire how beautiful it was if we hadn't been so worried about Tommy.

Shadowed by gray jagged mountains on all sides, the lake was like a volcano crater filled with moon-rippled water instead of lava. On the near shore of the lake, there was another stone table, illuminated by torches and portable camp lights.

Tommy's altar.

But he wasn't on it.

He was chained to an ancient stone pillar on the lakeshore.

"I've got the keys, Tommy boy!" sneered Chet Collier, who had a clinking key ring clipped to his belt.

"You're just trying to take me out of the game," said Tommy with a laugh, "because you crashed and burned with Q'orianka back in that village, after the flood. You can't stand the competition. I'm way hotter than you."

"You won't be hot tomorrow, Thomas," said Chet, sneering. "You'll be cold because you'll be dead."

The keys at his belt jingling like a wind chime, he stomped over to his father, crossing his arms and pouting like an angry toddler.

Collier's army of goons, all six of them, were patrolling the perimeter of their campsite. But none of them had weapons. They'd all left their rifles back at the temple.

DO ANY OF YOU GUYS HAVE HAIR GEL? MY HAIR GOT MUSSED ON THE MOTORCYCLE RIDE.
I WISH WE STIL HAD OUR RIFLES.
IF ANYBODY ATTACKS, WE'LL FIGHT CAVEMAN-STYLE. WE'LL FLING STONES AT 'EM.

The stone walls ringing the lake acted like an echo chamber, carrying Nathan Collier's taunts up to our hiding place.

"By rescuing your sister, you have helped us a great deal, Thomas!" said Collier.

"A captured warrior!" said his son Chet. "That's a way better sacrifice than your annoying sister."

Chains rattled. Tommy was fighting against his shackles.

"Back off, Chester," shouted Tommy. "Don't you dare disrespect my little sister."

"Little? She's huge!"

"I said back off!"

"Or what?" Chet laughed. "What are you going to do about it, Tailspin Tommy? I'll tell you what: Nothing! Especially after the high priest rips out your heart first thing tomorrow morning."

"Doesn't matter, dude. Heart or no heart, I will hunt you down. I will make you pay for what you just said."

"You won't be able to!" said Chet with a laugh. "You'll be dead!"

"Says who besides you?"

"The American Heart Association. They don't recommend operating heavy machinery, walking, seeking revenge, or doing anything if you don't have a pulse."

"Oh. Guess I missed that brochure."

Tommy slumped down. The wannabe high priest guy, who probably slept in his feathered headgear, marched over to the Colliers. Supay was right behind him. He still had his knife.

"Is all as it should be?" he asked. "Have you made the necessary preparations for *capacocha?*"

"Yes, mighty Willaq Umu!" said Nathan Collier, using the ancient name for the high priest. "Tomorrow morning, when beams from the rising sun hit the Sacred Stone in the tip of your staff, which you must place here, precisely four cubits away from the altar—"

"What's a cubit?" asked the priest.

"Let's see," mumbled Chet, "I used to know what a cubit was. I think you have to take a number and cube it, so four cubits would be—"

"Six feet!" shouted his father.

"Exactly," said Chet. "Four cubed is six—"

"Never mind, mighty Willaq Umu," said Nathan Collier. "Simply place your rod here, in this hole I dug with the toe of my boot. At dawn, the sun rising in the east will shine through the Sacred Stone and pinpoint the precise location of the portal into the Lost City of Paititi!"

"Whoa," said Tommy. "You got that bit from *Raiders of the Lost Ark.* When Indiana Jones is down in the snake pit with, like, the model of the city and he has the staff of Ra and all of a sudden, the sun—"

"Silence!" screamed Collier, because Tommy (who sometimes watches the Raiders movies with me) had totally busted him.

"Gag him!" ordered Chet.

The goon squad did as they were told. Tommy was muffled.

But he'd just helped us learn something extremely valuable.

Nathan Collier had absolutely no idea how to make the Lost City of Gold rise up in the valley of the lake.

Then again, neither did we.

CHAPTER 67

"We'll worry about Paititi later," whispered Dad. "Now we have to focus on rescuing your brother. Before dawn."

"We should strike tonight," said Storm.

Dad nodded. "We will."

He scratched out our new battle plan in the dust with a stick. Fortunately, the moon was bright enough that we could see his doodles without turning on our flashlights and giving away our location.

"As we just heard, they don't have any weapons," said Dad.

"Except the knife that guy Supay is always carrying around," I countered.

"It's for the sacrificial rite," said Dad. "They won't want to sully it with blood in combat."

"Good," I said. "Because I don't want to sully it with my blood either."

"We're going to have to work as a team and strictly follow our individual assignments," Dad continued. "Something you guys haven't always been great at."

Beck and I looked at each other.

Remember when we were supposed to stay on the *Lost* and guard the Room while Mom, Dad, and Tommy went looking for treasure on Cocos Island?

You may have forgotten about that. Dad hadn't.

Then there was that time when Chaupi's village flooded and Beck and I went swimming after his son Yacu even though Dad specifically ordered us not to do anything so foolish.

(That one ended up being totally heroic, too.)

"We'll do better this time," said Beck.

"Way better," I added.

“Good,” said Storm. “Because Tommy’s life depends on it.”

“Here’s your first assignment, twins,” said Dad. “Steal the horses. During the distraction, Storm and I will go for Chet and the keys to Tommy’s shackles.”

“Don’t worry, Dad!” I said. “We’ll stick to the plan this time. We’ll steal their horses!” Then, after a beat, I asked, “What horses are we talking about here?”

“I didn’t see any horses either,” said Beck. “Do they have horses now?”

“He means the motorcycles,” said Storm. “It’s a metaphor.”

“Ohhhhh,” we said. “Got it.”

Hours later, Collier and his crew extinguished their torches and lanterns and crawled into their sleeping bags and blankets.

We waited another hour to make sure they were sound asleep.

Then, on Dad’s signal, the four of us slunk

down the steep stone steps that led into the valley. The chirps and croaks of tree frogs covered whatever sounds we might've made.

When we reached the foot of the steps, Beck and I slipped off to the right. Storm and Dad went left.

They were going for Chet Collier's key ring.

We were going for the ATVs!

CHAPTER 68

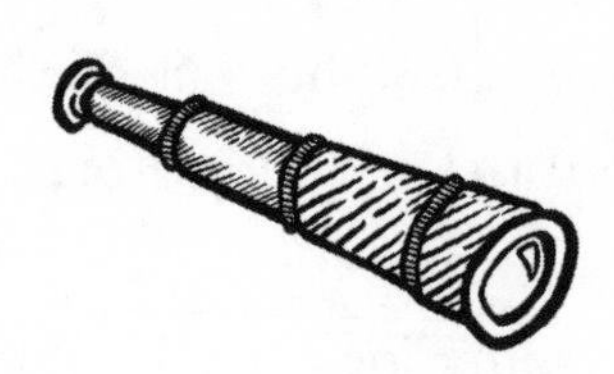

Beck and I raced across the Collier camp, heading for the motorbikes.

Dad and Storm went to Chet, who was fast asleep on a rolled-out blanket. Dad deftly removed the key ring from his belt. I think he learned pickpocketing when he went to CIA Spy School. He's scary-good at it. Especially for a parent.

Then they went over to the post where Tommy was chained—and wide awake, by the way.

Beck and I hopped on a pair of ATVs and kick-started them.

The instant they roared to life, we jumped on a different pair and got them revving, too.

The other two were for Dad and Tommy. Storm doesn't ATV. She'd hang on to Dad or Tommy.

"Who's stealing the ATVs this time?" screamed Nathan Collier, climbing out of his high-tech sleeping bag and patting his hair to make certain all his curls were locked in place.

"We are!" I shouted. "Catch us if you can, Collier!"

Oh, yeah. I really spat out that *K* sound.

Beck zoomed left. I zoomed right.

Not to brag, but both of us are awesome on ATVs!

I did a little of what's called *drifting* around the campsite. I spun my ride in circles with my rear tires slipping out to the side, which kicked up a ton of gritty dirt that sprayed all over the bad guys; they had to wipe their eyes even more than usual as they woke up.

Beck was up in a squat, keeping most of her weight toward the back of her ATV. I could tell she was about to execute a jump right over the high-priest dude. She gunned the throttle and bought some major-league air, sailing inches above the startled old guy.

The high priest was so stunned, I was able to swoop into a fishtail skid, buzz past, lean down, and snag his headpiece. On my second pass, I got the rod with the Sacred Stone locked into the golden corncob.

"Finders keepers," I shouted. "Losers weepers. Yee-haw!"

Beck and I whooped and hollered and put on an incredible display of ATV freestyle moves. It was more fun than a video game because it was real!

Meanwhile, Dad, Tommy, and Storm had charged across the clearing to the two quads we'd started for them. Dad and Storm hopped on one ATV, Tommy on the other. Beck and I circled back to the starting line and joined the Kidd family parade.

"Follow my lead!" shouted Dad.

"Yes, sir!" we all shouted back.

No way were we disobeying Dad again.

Although maybe we should've. He was kind of new to ATV riding.

He led us back to the steps we'd climbed down earlier.

ATVs aren't great on steps or staircases. You have to pop a wheelie for every single step you're trying to climb.

Dad made it up just one before his engine died.

Something we were all about to do.

Because Collier's goons were maybe ten yards behind us.

Supay, too.

And he had that knife.

CHAPTER 69

"New plan!" Dad shouted.

"Chya," said Tommy. "We totally need one."

Dad, with Storm's arms still wrapped around his waist, leaped up and came down hard on his starter. His ATV's engine sprang back to life.

"Reverse course," said Dad. "Skirt the edge of the lake. Bick, Beck, take the lead. There has to be another way out of this valley!"

"On it!" I shouted, since I was on the bike in the rear, which would now be the lead.

I did a 180 doughnut, spewing pebbles as I went.

"Thanks a lot, Bick," said Beck, who was behind me, eating my dust and pebbles.

She swung sideways, too, and pelted Tommy with gravel. Tommy's backwash hit Dad and Storm. Like they always say: The family that sprays together stays together.

When we were relined up, I saw that Supay had sheathed his knife and was taking care of the high priest. I guess Beck's jump had nearly given him a heart attack, which was kind of ironic since he wanted to attack Tommy's heart. Meanwhile, Collier's goons raced forward. They didn't have rifles, just rocks, which they flung at me.

A stone the size of a softball dinged me on the shoulder.

"Ouch!" I hollered as I popped a wheelie and went flying forward on my rear wheels, turning the ATV undercarriage into a shield and a wedge. It protected me from being beaned by any more stones. It also split the bad guys apart because none of them wanted to be run over by a seriously enraged Kidd kid they'd just whacked on the shoulder with a jumbo-size rock!

"Ride along the edge of the lake, Bick," shouted Beck from behind me once I'd cleared the field. "I see an opening on the far side."

"I see it, too!" I said.

(Note to self: In the future, try to schedule all getaway chase scenes during daylight hours.)

We were whipping around the shoreline of the moonlit lake. I was kind of marveling at how this rocky crater seemed to appear out of nowhere in the middle of the Peruvian rain forest. It was almost as if it were man-made, like a lagoon at Disney World.

I didn't get to marvel for long.

I heard a *bong,* like a rubber band snapping.

The *bong* was followed by a *thwick.* Then another *bong.* More *thwick*s. A few *boing-bong*s and then a shower of *thwickety-thwick-thwick-thwick*s!

Tiny darts shot out of all the crevices in the craggy rock walls lining the lake. I dodged a bunch of them but at least four of them punctured my tires.

I stood up and whirled around.

Beck was getting nailed by flying darts, too. The barrage was so thick, it looked like a swarm of angry wasps. Tommy and Dad were bobbing and weaving on their dirt bikes, trying to avoid the pointy projectiles, but they weren't winning the darts game either. Before long, all of us were bumping along on nothing but rims, our tires totally deflated.

And then another mosquito bit me in the neck.

Except that this time, I realized it wasn't a blood-sucking winged insect.

I knew it was a wooden dart dipped in something nasty.

In a flash, I fell asleep at the wheel.

Literally.

The last thing I remember is toppling off the ATV seat and landing in the dirt with my head resting on a flat tire.

CHAPTER 70

Our great escape turned out to be not so great.

When whatever the dart drug was wore off (around five a.m.), we all woke up to discover that we'd been chained together, with our hands cuffed behind us, at the base of an ancient Incan idol—a weird smiling guy with a slit for a mouth.

"Was this thing here last night?" I asked through a yawn.

"Chya," said Tommy. "Collier wanted to chain me to it but the dude with the feathers said he couldn't. Said it was a sacred sculpture."

“Who’s it supposed to be?” asked Beck, our family artiste.

“Feather Head called him Inkarri,” said Tommy.

“Inkarri,” said Dad pensively. That meant he was thinking about stuff. Dad does that a lot. “The statue’s presence is further proof that the Lost City of Paititi is close at hand.”

I squirmed around a little and noticed something kind of odd.

The old guy, the mighty Willaq Umu or whatever, the wannabe-high-priest dude, was sitting on the ground, chained to the post where Tommy had been chained. His buddy Supay was chained right beside him. The high priest wasn't wearing his robes or his feathered hat. Just antique underpants.

"What's going on?" I muttered.

"Good question," said Dad. "I suspect Collier no longer thinks he needs those two gentlemen to help him raise Paititi from its hiding place. His ego is such that he thinks he can do it all by himself. And here is something else for us to ponder: Those dart guns that did us in last night weren't installed by Nathan Collier or his crew. Remember, they only just discovered this site last night. There was no time for them to engineer a defensive contraption as complex as the trip-wire dart-gun artillery installation we encountered."

"So who put the dart-launcher things in all the

rocks?" asked Tommy. "There were like a bajillion of them, all firing at once."

"My guess?" said Dad, looking up at the smiling idol behind us. "Inkarri's followers. Five hundred years ago."

"They installed the same kind of defenses here that Beck and I discovered in that cave back at the necropolis!" I said.

Dad nodded. "Such is my supposition."

"So those darts were dipped in, like, a five-hundred-year-old sleeping potion?" asked Tommy.

"Powerful stuff," said Storm. "But I suspect its potency has diminished over the centuries. If we had come by, oh, two hundred years ago, we'd probably all be dead right now."

"Great," I said. "Another lucky break."

"Now if only we could stop the sun from rising," said Beck, nodding her head toward the eastern sky, which was starting to glow golden.

Dawn was about to break.

So were our rib cages.

CHAPTER 71

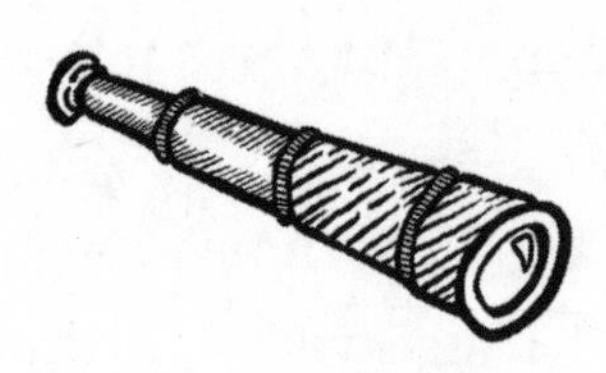

I squinted at the rising sun as the silhouette of a short, stubby figure—made slightly taller by the high priest's feathered headpiece, sitting lopsided on his head—emerged from the shadows.

He was using the golden corncob staff as a walking stick. The stick was twice as tall as he was. He was wearing some kind of long robe or dress. It was two sizes too big for his tiny frame, so the fabric sort of puddled around his ankles.

Nathan and Chet Collier stepped out of the darkness to flank him.

"The sun god smiles on us this day!" said the short man in a very thick Spanish accent. "We have five hearts to choose from for our sacrificial rite of *capacocha!*"

"That's true, Señor Rojas," said Nathan Collier, sounding like a total suck-up. "If at first we don't succeed, we can try, try again!"

"Shut up, Nathan," said the man in the middle without turning to look at either Collier. "Or I will send you and your son away as I sent away your worthless soldiers of fortune."

"You betcha, Señor Rojas. Zipping my lip. I'm only here to help. Got the whole sacrificial rite memorized. Won't say a word until we're ready to go full-on *capacocha*."

"Nathan?"

"*Sí,* señor?"

"Shut! Up!"

"Right. No problemo. Shutting up."

I checked out as much of the surrounding area as I could with my arms pinned behind my back. The goons were definitely gone. It was just the two Colliers; the high priest and Supay chained to Tommy's old post; us chained to the Inkarri statue; and Señor Rojas. His name, of course, rang a bell. A very loud bell.

"Juan Carlos Rojas," said Dad calmly. "At long last, we meet."

"Yes. Too bad your wife isn't here, Dr. Kidd. Then I could kill you all in one swell foop!"

"You mean 'one fell swoop,'" said Storm. "When studying English as a second language, a command of common euphemisms and expressions can prove quite useful."

"*¡Silencio!* Oh, how I wish Mrs. Kidd and that idiot Chaupi were here. I would cut out their hearts first. Dragging me to that ridiculous summit meeting at the presidential palace in Lima. Meddling in my affairs. Trying to take away what is rightfully mine."

"And what would that be?" asked Dad, because he's not afraid of anybody or anything, including Supay's knife, which Juan Carlos Rojas had just pulled out of the fancy belt tied around his shiny priest robe.

"The rain forest!"

"You don't own it, Señor Rojas."

"Perhaps not," he said with a grin. "But soon I will. I will own the entire country. The people of Peru will gratefully give me everything I desire!" He was sounding loonier and loonier as he gestured to the old high priest and Supay. "For I will prove to those two ignorant peasants that I, Juan Carlos Rojas, am the new sun god! I will command the Lost City of Paititi to rise from its tomb, and, with Señor Collier's magical words and your human hearts as a sacrificial offering, it will do my bidding! After such a feat, who would dare stand in my way? When I restore Paititi to its former glory, all will call me Inkarri! They will crown me the new king of the Incas! I will rule the rain forest!"

CHAPTER 72

Nathan Collier went over to the stone slab and sprinkled it with dry leaves.

I think it was cilantro. The air suddenly smelled like salsa.

"I am now preparing the sacrificial altar for *capacocha!*" he declared.

"I am now sharpening the blade on my sacrificial knife!" cried Juan Carlos Rojas.

"I am now standing over here," said Chet who probably figured he was supposed to say something.

I really did wish Mom were there. Just so I could say good-bye. Just so we could all be together again. Just so I could apologize for every time I did something stupid or didn't play my part and do what the family needed me to do.

Rojas slipped the blade back into his belt, thrust out his arms, and raised them high.

"Bring unto me the sacrificial child!" he said to the sky.

"We should start with that one," said Chet, pointing at Tommy. "He's such a brave warrior, all the ladies looooove him."

"Very well," said Rojas. "Bring him forth unto the altar!"

Chet and Nathan Collier bustled over to where we all sat at the base of the golden idol. Mr. Collier pointed his pistol at Beck's head.

"One false move, Thomas," he said, "and I will shoot your little sister."

Chet slipped the chain through Tommy's handcuffs and grabbed him roughly by the arm.

He forgot to relock the chain.

The two Colliers dragged Tommy over to the altar.

"Whoa, take it easy, dudes. You're messing up my hair again."

"That won't matter where you're going," said Chet. "There won't be any girls!"

"What? How can it be heaven if there aren't any angels?"

"Quiet!" shouted Rojas. "This is a religious service. Show some respect."

"Sorry," said Tommy. "My bad."

The three men hoisted him up onto the stone table and forced him to lie down.

"On my *go*," whispered Dad, because even though we were still handcuffed, there was nothing securing us to the idol's legs anymore. We could rush Rojas and head-butt him until he dropped the blade.

"Say the words, Mr. Collier!" said Señor Rojas. "Begin the ritual. It is time for *capacocha!*"

Nathan Collier looked nervous. For his whole career, he'd made his name and fame by mooching off other people. He never did any real work or any homework. My guess? He had no idea what words he was supposed to speak.

So he improvised.

"Inca, dinka, pinka, doo! Arise, O Paititi, as I command you to."

Rojas lowered his priestly arms and stared at Collier.

"What are you gibbering about? What are those silly words?"

"It's a rough translation of the, uh, ancient text," explained Collier. "But don't worry. If it doesn't work with this Kidd, we have four more to choose from."

"Fine," said Rojas, raising his knife high above his head, getting ready to plunge it deep into Tommy's chest. "Continue!"

"Don't you dare!" shouted a woman from the ridge above us.

"Leave Tommy alone!" shouted another.

I looked up.

It was Q'orianka and Milagros, the two beautiful girls Tommy had fallen in love with on this adventure. Apparently the feeling was mutual.

"Don't you dare harm my son!"

Mom was up there on the bluff, too! Chaupi was right beside her. Mom had a video camera on her shoulder. She was also accompanied by what looked like a couple hundred indigenous people. From the village with the flood. And from the tribe near the river and the giant anaconda.

Well, what do you know?

Mom had arrived just in time and she'd brought along the cavalry.

WHO INVITED ALL THESE NATIVES?
?
!!!
ME. THEY'RE MY KIND OF PEOPLE. INDIGENOUS.

CHAPTER 73

"Take him down, Yacu!" commanded Chaupi, the leader of the flooded village we'd visited.

"Yes, Father!"

Up on the ridge, the little boy Yacu, the one Beck and I had saved, held up an enormous blowgun. The thing had to be two yards long. Yacu? He was maybe three feet tall. Juan Carlos Rojas stared at the boy in disbelief.

"Who are these insolent jackals?" he bellowed. "Do they not know who I am? Why are they not bowing down before me?"

While he was distracted, Tommy rolled off the altar.

Yacu took his shot.

I heard something whizzing through the air and then the telltale *fwick!* of a dart hitting flesh.

"Yoooow!" shrieked Juan Carlos Rojas, dropping the knife and raising a hand to his neck to slap whatever had just bitten him.

It was a dart, of course. With fast-acting sleepy-time juice on its tip.

Rojas's knees buckled. His shoulders drooped. His feathered crown toppled off his head. He crumpled to the ground to become a lumpy heap of priest robe.

Little Yacu had totally nailed him. The kid had some pair of lungs.

"Now!" shouted Dad.

Beck, Storm, Dad, and I charged across the clearing and rammed both Colliers in their guts as Mom and her war-cry-whooping army of locals streamed down from the ridge into the valley.

The battle was over in, like, fifteen seconds.

"Sorry we couldn't attack sooner," said Mom after she and Dad had kissed and we'd all hugged and junk. "Chaupi and I wanted to get video of Señor Rojas poised to strike Tommy with the knife. It's all the evidence we need. I feel certain he will now be charged with attempted murder."

"What about the Colliers?" I said, spitting out that crummy *K* sound again.

"They're going to jail, too," said Mom.

"On what charge?" fumed Nathan Collier, who

was being restrained by six beefy residents of Chaupi's village.

"Conspiracy to commit murder!" snarled Mom.

"Nuh-uh," whimpered Chet, also being restrained by half a dozen musclemen. "It wasn't murder, Mrs. Kidd. We were doing archaeological research on the ancient Incan custom of child sacrifice."

"Tell it to the judge," said Dad.

"Chya," said Tommy. "Maybe he'll let you off with a warning. Not!"

Chaupi ripped the key chain off Chet's belt and freed us all from our shackles.

"Are you injured, Tommy?" asked Milagros, who'd come tearing down into the valley with Mom and the rest of the cavalry.

"Did these mean men hurt you?" cooed Q'ori-anka. Both girls were kind of rubbing Tommy's muscles and stuff, trying to soothe and comfort him. It was gross.

"It hurt a little bit," said Tommy. He pointed to his lips. "Right around here."

Beck and I tried not to hurl.

TO TOTALLY RECOVER, I THINK I'M GOING TO NEED SEVERAL HOURS OF INTENSIVE LIP THERAPY.
Z-Z-Z-Z

A Peruvian army helicopter landed in the clearing to cart Rojas, the high priest, Supay, and the Colliers away.

We were all feeling great. Storm was actually smiling.

But not Dad. He looked bummed.

"I really thought, at the end of this journey, we'd find the Lost City of Gold," he muttered.

"Professor Thomas Kidd?" scoffed Mom. "Don't tell me you're giving up before the quest is over. What kind of treasure hunter are you, anyway?"

She was grinning.

She definitely had something up her sleeve.

And I couldn't wait to see what it was!

CHAPTER 74

"While I was in Lima," Mom explained, "the president granted Chaupi and me access to two treasures from the archives of their National Museum of Archaeology, Anthropology, and History."

"What are they?" I asked.

"The first," said Mom, "is a very short sermon from our old friend Father Toledo. It was meant to be sent to His Holiness the Pope in Rome, but, for whatever reason, it never was."

"What does it say?" asked Dad.

Mom handed the piece of weathered parchment, which was hermetically sealed in a plastic sleeve, to Storm, because she can speed-translate from Spanish to English.

"Looks like a riddle," said Storm.

"That's what I thought, too," said Mom.

Storm read it out loud: "'To find the treasure, follow Romans twelve-five, for it is how Inkarri will one day be put back together. When he is, the City of Gold will not rise, but it shall be found. Romans twelve-five is the key and it must be turned where the pagan idol still smiles like an innocent child.'"

"I did some homework on the chopper flight up," said Mom. "Romans twelve-five, of course, refers to a verse in the Bible: 'So we, though many, form one body.'"

"Cool," I said. "But what does it mean?"

"Well, I'm not a biblical scholar—"

"You just have to finish writing that one paper, Sue, and you will be," said Dad.

"True. But I think the verse means that the early Church, being described by Saint Paul in that verse, is sort of like our family. Everybody brings different talents to the table but we all need each other to be whole and complete."

"Well, if I may," said Storm, "how does that help us find the Lost City of Paititi?"

Mom held up a finger. "Aha. Item number two from the museum."

She pulled a bundle of purple velvet out of her knapsack, unwrapped the cloth, and revealed the rounded blade of a *tumi* knife attached to a flat plate with several bumps and grooves arrayed across its body with geometric precision. It kind of reminded me of a circuit board where you pop computer components into place.

Something was etched into the metal plate in ancient Incan script—the same kind of writing we'd seen on the cave wall where we found the Sacred Stone.

"What's it say?" asked Beck.

"'I am Inkarri,'" translated Storm.

"Tom," Mom said to Dad, "remember that *tumi* piece you found on Cocos Island?"

"The head," said Dad, reaching into his pocket and pulling out the carved piece of gold. He handed it to Mom. She put it down at the top of the flat plate.

It snapped into place!

Chaupi stepped forward. "Only one with great intelligence could find Inkarri's head, his seat of wisdom, which long ago had been entrusted to the good priest Father Toledo."

"Of course!" blurted out Storm. "The legend of Inkarri! It all makes sense."

Okay. Maybe to her.

But I was still kind of in the dark.

CHAPTER 75

"Remember?" said Storm. "The conquistadors chopped Inkarri's body into a bunch of pieces. His head was buried one place, his arms and legs and torso somewhere else."

"Yes," said Chaupi. "For the Spaniards feared Inkarri's vow to rise from the dead."

"And if his body was ever reconstructed," said Dad, "if all the pieces were put back together, the Incan Empire would rise from the ashes."

"The same is true for the sacred *tumi,*" said Chaupi. "Inkarri's followers scattered its pieces all over the rain forest. They trusted our ancestors who lived in remote isolation to guard and protect these precious artifacts across the centuries. We were to give them only to people like Father Toledo, individuals who, because of their goodness and strength of character, could be trusted to return our hidden treasure to us once it was found. Explorers with cunning, courage, wisdom, and, most important, compassion."

Storm handed Mom her golden rectangle. The *tumi*'s chest and tummy.

"You carry the heart," Chaupi told Storm. "For you are brave and have a courageous heart."

"Maybe," said Storm, blushing a little. "I mean, I didn't totally freak out when they hauled me away and threatened to cut out my heart. I just tried to hide the treasure map carved into the altar."

Dad draped his arm around Storm. "You are very brave indeed."

The torso snapped into place on the *tumi* plate.

"We got the feet," I said, and Beck and I handed our necklaces to Mom.

"For you two," said Chaupi, "ran bravely into danger when others would have flown in the opposite direction."

"True," said Beck. "Guess that's our superpower—doing crazy stuff we probably shouldn't."

Mom placed the feet on the plate. They fit perfectly.

"And Milagros's dad gave me these," said Tommy. "They sort of look like wings."

"Because you flew with wings of courage to rescue my youngest daughter," said Milagros's grateful father. "With no regard for your own safety."

"Well," said Tommy, "I did have that Snake Attack 101 course that Dad taught..."

Mom added the two wings to the sides of the torso.

The *tumi* was complete.

Inkarri had been put back together.

"So," I said, looking around, "he's all back together. Where's the gold?"

"The *tumi* is the key, Bick," said Mom. "Now we need to find the keyhole."

POOR INKARRI. IT LOOKS LIKE HE HAS INDIGESTION. OR GAS. MAYBE BOTH.

"Um, how about that guy?" said Beck, pointing at the grinning golden idol.

"Of course!" said Dad.

Mom slid the *tumi* deep into the idol's smile slot. The only thing still sticking out was the crown, just like on a door key!

"You turn it, Tommy," said Mom. "I'm too nervous."

Tommy gave the thing a good strong twist.

All of a sudden, I heard stone sliding against stone again—just like when the walls opened back at the necropolis!

CHAPTER 76

The grinding noises grew louder.

The earth beneath our feet started to rumble.

I thought that part of Peru might be having an earthquake.

"There!" shouted Beck, pointing to the far edge of the lake. "The stones are falling away."

"Actually," said Storm, "they are sliding down, much like the floodgates opening on a dam."

Water started gushing out of the lake. White,

choppy rapids furiously sluiced over the stone wall on the distant shore.

"It's a man-made lake," I shouted. "Just like the lagoon at Disney World!"

"Inkarri's followers built a dam," said Dad excitedly. "The monsoons of the rain forest must have filled the lake, and they've kept the Lost City of Gold hidden underwater for centuries."

"Look!" shouted Mom. "The peak of a pyramid! It's just like Father Toledo said. 'The City of Gold will not rise, but it shall be found.'"

"When the waters of the lake recede!" added Dad. "The rains of the rain forest have protected the Incas' treasure for centuries! How ingenious the Incas were!"

"Now," said Mom, "it's time for all that gold to return the favor and help save the rain forest for their descendants."

And then all of us just stood there in awe as the water drained out of the lake and the hidden city was slowly revealed, its golden peaks and spires gleaming in the sun.

I THINK THOSE BUILDINGS ARE MADE OF GOLD BRICKS!
WOW! IT'S LIKE FINDING BURIED TREASURE UNDER THE OCEAN!
BUT WITHOUT HAVING TO GO SCUBA DIVING.
GOOD THING GOLD DOESN'T RUST.

By noon, the baking heat of the sun had dried out the streets and golden pyramids of the lost city.

Mom called the president of Peru on our satellite phone.

"That trust for rain-forest protection that we discussed has been fully funded, Your Excellency. Can you send an extraction team to these coordinates to evaluate your newfound gold? And, sir? It should be a big team. A very big team."

While we waited for the Peruvian officials to arrive, we threw a little fiesta on the bluffs overlooking the City of Gold. There was drum, guitar, and flute music. We had corn cakes and popcorn and corn fritters. Tommy danced with every girl he could. Storm pointed out interesting architectural details sculpted into the golden city's turrets and towers.

Mom and Dad were happy that we had taken one more step toward saving the most precious treasure on the planet—Earth itself.

Beck and me?

Well, we thought about launching into another Twin Tirade.

But then we realized we were just too darn happy to do it.

So what's next for the Kidd Family Treasure Hunters?

I'm not sure.

Maybe Forrest Fenn's million-dollar buried treasure, rumored to be hidden somewhere in the Rocky Mountains. Then there are stories about a lost Spanish galleon loaded with black pearls buried beneath the sands of the Mojave Desert. Or how about the Lost Dutchman's Gold Mine in Arizona?

Well, whatever treasure we hunt for next, one thing's for sure: We'll find it a lot faster if we all work together!

HUNTING FOR YOUR NEXT THRILLING ADVENTURE?

We're Bick and Beck Kidd,
treasure hunters extraordinaire!
It's so cool being part of a family that sails around the world, looking for amazing artifacts and being chased by bad guys.
You don't want to miss a single one of our epic adventures around the world!

JOIN US! READ THE WHOLE TREASURE HUNTERS SERIES.

Grrrrg-bloop.

What's that? A weird, gurgling noise is coming from the shower. I walk over to the clear-glass door and open it. Everything looks okay. I don't smell anything, either.

I bend all the way over until my face is next to the drain, and that's when I pick up just a trace of something—

CLAAAANG!

The drain cover flies off. Before I know what's happening, long, spaghetti-like tentacles explode through the hole and wrap themselves around my head! Instinctively, I lunge backward, but they tighten and force my face to the floor. I feel them squeezing me, cutting off the circulation to my brain. In a desperate move, I put my hands on the floor and do the longest, most painful push-up of my life. The tentacles stretch, and an instant later, my head is free. I rocket backward, collapsing against the shower wall.

But just when I think it's over, four small, smelly creatures crawl out of the drain.

They're disgusting. I mean really disgusting. They look like squishy bowling balls with party streamers for legs. I jump to my feet and try to run, but a web of spidery tentacles clutches my knee-caps. There's a sudden yank, and I go crashing against the side of a tall wooden cabinet, toppling it to the floor. The creatures swarm me like bees.

Quickly, I reach behind me and feel something cool and dangerous—Big Joe's hammer. I swing wild, but get lucky. The hammer head connects with one of the jelly-beasts, sending it flying against a laundry hamper.

"Sully! Sully!"

It's Big Joe. He's pounding on the bathroom door, but the overturned cabinet is wedged against it. Before I can say anything, a squish-monster attaches itself to my face. Ewwwwwww! It smells like the inside of a bait bucket. I pry it loose and fling the thing into the sink. Then I bring the hammer down.

Unfortunately, the sucker is as quick as it is

ugly. It moves, and I whack the shiny, chrome faucet instead. A tall stream of water gushes into the air. Swatting like an insane carpenter, I chase the three remaining creatures back into the shower.

The silver hammer is nothing but a blur as I take out two showerheads, some Italian tiles, and an innocent soap dish. I must have broken a couple of pipes because water is flooding the bathroom floor. Everywhere I look, there are bouncing blobs and tentacles striking at me like snakes. I lose my balance and fall through the shower door, shattering it into a million pieces.

"Sully!"

That's weird...I hear Big Joe's voice, but it seems strange and far away. Everything does. It's almost as if the world outside this room has disappeared, and nothing is left but me and the squishees. I don't know, maybe it's the fear, or the anger, or my possible concussion, but all of a sudden I feel different—like someone just connected a loose wire in my brain. Without thinking, I snatch a floating screwdriver out of the water and hurl it through the air. It spins a dozen times before nailing one of the blobs to the wall. I snag a second creature in a bath towel, and slingshot it against the ceiling.

That means there's just one monster left—and it's streaking right toward me. Moving on instinct, I roll out of the way, grab the toilet plunger, and bat the thing like Babe Ruth hitting a homer. The blast splatters it against the back of the toilet, and it ricochets into the bowl.

Quickly, I slam the lid down, and leap on top of it.

A few seconds later, the overturned cabinet scoots across the wet tiles, and Big Joe and Izzy come bursting through the door. I don't know what they're thinking, but I know what they see: spewing water pipes, broken fixtures, shattered glass, and a crazed thirteen-year-old standing on a toilet seat with a bath towel cape and a mighty plunger raised in triumph.

"Smile," Izzy says.

Then she points her phone, and clicks.

JAMES PATTERSON holds the Guinness World Record for the most #1 *New York Times* bestsellers, including *Middle School*, *I Funny*, and *Jacky Ha-Ha*, and his books have sold more than 350 million copies worldwide. A tireless champion of the power of books and reading, Patterson created a children's book imprint, JIMMY Patterson, whose mission is simple: "We want every kid who finishes a JIMMY Book to say, 'PLEASE GIVE ME ANOTHER BOOK.'" He has donated more than one million books to students and soldiers and funds over four hundred Teacher Education Scholarships at twenty-four colleges and universities. He has also donated millions of dollars to independent bookstores and school libraries. Patterson invests proceeds from the sales of JIMMY Patterson Books in pro-reading initiatives.

CHRIS GRABENSTEIN is a *New York Times* bestselling author who has collaborated with James Patterson on the I Funny, Treasure Hunters, and House of Robots series, as well as *Jacky Ha-Ha*, *Word of Mouse*, *Pottymouth and Stupid*, *Laugh Out Loud*, and *Daniel X: Armageddon*. He lives in New York City.

JULIANA NEUFELD is an award-winning illustrator who has also worked with James Patterson on the Treasure Hunters and the House of Robots series. Her drawings can be found in books, on album covers, and in nooks and crannies throughout the internet. She lives in Toronto.

BACK OFF, BOYS! I'M STORM! YOUR ONE-WOMAN SHARKNADO!
CAN DEFINITELY
LADIES SEE IN ME.
WOW!
RATTLE RATTLE RATTLE